Capricious Demise

Shandra Higheagle Mystery
Book 15

Paty Jager

Windtree Press
Hillsboro, Oregon

Special Thanks to:

Judy Melinek, M.D.

Bob Mueller

Chapter One

Two children, a boy and a girl, stood on a ledge on a mountain, crying. Shandra jumped off her horse and ran to the base of the mountain and began clawing her way up the cliff. Grandmother sat on a rock, nodding and pointing at the children. Shandra's fingernails grew into claws as she slipped backwards on the rock and called out to the children not to be afraid.

"Wake up. Shandra, wake up."

Shaking jostled Shandra Higheagle Greer awake. She stared into the eyes of her husband, Ryan. But her mind still saw the children crying on the ledge and her heart still pounded with fear. "We have to help them," she beseeched her husband.

"Help who?" He now held her in his arms. "You cried out, 'I'm coming!' Who were you trying to reach?"

"Two children on a ledge. Grandmother was there,

nodding and pointing at the children." She relaxed in his arms and as always happened after a dream where her deceased grandmother showed herself, Shandra began decrypting what had happened.

"Grandmother wanted me to save the children—a boy and girl. They looked young. Around six or seven, maybe. But where are they and how do I save them?" She shoved out of Ryan's embrace and stared into his eyes. "Are they lost, missing, is someone abusing them?" Her chest squeezed with the fear she'd felt while in the dream.

"I'll check the missing children lists in the morning when I get to work. Go back to sleep." Ryan settled her back down on the bed, but she couldn't get the two children out of her mind.

Once Ryan fell back to sleep, she slipped out of his arms, pulled on a robe, and wandered out to the kitchen with Sheba, her pony-sized half Newfoundland and half Border Collie, at her heels. She made a cup of chamomile tea and sat on the couch, stroking Sheba's head, and worrying about the two children she didn't know. She had an intense desire to save and nurture the two. "They must be coming into our lives," she said to Sheba. Ella only showed up in her dreams when there was a murder to solve. Shandra sent up prayers to the Creator that it wasn't the two children.

After Ruthie and Maxwell Treat, her best friend and her husband, had little Donnie, she and Ryan had started talking about children. At her age a pregnancy would be tough on both herself and a baby, but so far Ryan's brother, Conor, and his wife, Lissa, hadn't provided a male heir to the Greer name, making her father-in-law put more pressure on the two boys. The

Greer women had provided five grandchildren but, of course, their last names weren't Greer.

Shandra pulled her laptop onto her lap and began looking online for stories of missing children in the surrounding newspapers. She dozed off and on, finally putting the laptop on the table and getting off the couch.

Ryan walked into the kitchen as she made another cup of tea. She walked over to the coffee pot and started it.

"Did you sleep at all after your dream?" he asked, pulling her into his arms.

"A little here and there. I looked up all the local newspapers and there haven't been any reports of missing children." She moved from his embrace and poured Ryan a cup of coffee. "What worries me is, if they are in danger, how do we know where to find them? They were on a ledge on a mountainside. I was riding my horse." She stopped and stared at Ryan. "Do you think they are lost on Huckleberry Mountain?"

Ryan took the cup of coffee from her and gently moved her to a stool at the island. "Sit. I'll make breakfast and you write down everything you remember from your dream."

That's what she loved about her husband. He'd believed in her dreams before she had. They'd solved over a dozen murders with her dreams that included her deceased grandmother, a member of the Nez Perce tribe from the Colville Reservation in Washington State. However, Ella never gave them anything straight forward. They always had to decipher the meaning of what she showed. This time, Shandra understood, she would help the children. But how? To find them? To save them?

As she made a list of what she remembered from the dream, the back door opened and the clomp of her employee's boots thumped down the hall to the kitchen.

Shandra glanced up. The sadness on the woman's face said it all. She slipped off the stool and put an arm around Lil's shoulders. "Sunshine left us?"

"She was the best danged mare I've ever had. I held her head in my lap all night, tryin' to ease her pain." Lil stepped out of the one-armed hug, sniffed, and walked over to the coffeemaker.

"Sorry to hear about Sunshine," Ryan said.

"Humph," was Lil's reply.

While her cantankerous employee, who'd come with the ranch like a stray cat, had not liked Ryan in the beginning, they had learned to get along. They had bonded over their love of Shandra. But there were also times when she saw, that while they tossed barbs at one another, Ryan and Lil had become friends.

"Where do you want to bury her?" Shandra asked, glad to have something to take her mind off the children, but sad for her friend who had had the mare for over thirty years. They both knew this day was coming. She'd tried to talk Lil into getting another mare so she'd have something to take Sunshine's place, but Lil said she wouldn't do that until her mare was in the ground. She didn't want Sunshine to think she wasn't loved because she was old.

Which Shandra took as a metaphor for Lil's own life.

"I know it would be hard to get her up there, bein's there could still be some snow, but I'd like her to be up with my baby." Lil gave her a furtive glance. It was rare she talked about the child she'd miscarried over forty years ago.

"I'll make some phone calls and see if we can get Arnold Hulse to bring his equipment out today." Shandra walked over to the drawer where she kept the local directory of businesses.

"Do you mind if I ride Oliver up and mark the spot, then go to town while Sunshine's bein' buried?" Lil held the cup of coffee in front of her face.

Shandra had a feeling the crusty old woman who had a heart of gold was having trouble keeping herself together.

"I don't see a problem with that, but you might want to take Duke, he's younger for that climb. Especially if there is still snow up there. It is the middle of April and we had a good snowpack."

"Duke is Ryan's horse," Lil said.

"He's only the horse I ride. He isn't mine. He belongs to Shandra. Take Duke. I'd hate for Arnold to have to bury two horses today," Ryan said.

Shandra smacked him on the shoulder with the directory.

"What?" he stared at her.

"That wasn't very sympathetic." Shandra sat down at the counter and opened the directory.

Lil put the cup of coffee down. "I'll go saddle Duke. I'll come by when I get back, let you know the conditions, and see if someone will be taking care of Sunshine today."

"Take your time on the mountain." Shandra wanted to add, check all the ledges for stray children.

After the door closed, Ryan put a plate of scrambled eggs and diced ham in front of her. "I've always known Lil was contrary, but to think Oliver would make it up to that spot on the mountain was wishful thinking."

Shandra stared at him. "When you said Oliver wouldn't make it, you might as well have been saying Lil should stay off a horse and sit in a rocking chair. Remember, she is getting close to the age of Oliver and Sunshine in people years."

Ryan sat down beside her with his own plate. "I didn't mean it that way. Just that Oliver hasn't been ridden much and would be out of shape, not to mention his age."

Shandra shook her head at how insensitive her husband could be at times and shoved the list of things she remembered about the dream over to him as she dug into her breakfast. This was going to be a hard day with as little sleep as she had and getting Lil's horse buried.

Chapter Two

It was rare that Shandra's dreams involving her grandmother didn't turn into something that helped Ryan with solving cases, but this time he wasn't sure what it meant. He'd checked all missing children lists from the whole state of Idaho and the surrounding states. Nothing fit the descriptions of the two children she saw in her dream. He had to be evasive when Sheriff Oldham asked him why he was looking up missing children. If the sheriff's department knew he'd solved so many murders due to help from his wife's dreams, he'd be laughed out of a job.

Sheriff Oldham walked into the small room that had become Ryan's office a year after he joined the Weippe County Sheriff's Department as a detective. "A suicide's been called in. It's on the way to South Tucker campground. Gerald is already there."

Ryan turned the monitor off on his computer,

grabbed his coat and hat, and headed to his SUV.

On the drive, he kept thinking about Shandra's dream and wondering if Arnold would be able to bury the horse where Lil wanted it. As much as he and the crusty old woman knocked heads, he would do everything in his power to make her life easier because Shandra loved the woman like an aunt.

He could tell the children in Shandra's dream had rattled her. He didn't know if it was because they had been talking about starting a family or because of what she saw. He knew she'd told him everything about the dream, but he was pretty sure when she woke, she couldn't remember every detail that tugged at her emotions while she was sleeping.

Deputy Speaks car sat at the end of two hundred yards of muddy dirt road off the county highway. The lights were flashing and two dogs were barking.

Ryan parked beside the patrol car, grabbed his crime scene pack, and stepped out of the vehicle. The two mid-sized, mixed mutt dogs ran at him, their teeth bared and snarling.

"Pike, Rambo, get back here!" a man in a plaid jacket and matching hat yelled. The two dogs spun around so fast, their noses touched their tails and they ran back to the man.

"Thanks," Ryan said, walking toward the man. "Weippe County Detective Ryan Greer." He held out a hand to shake.

The man looked at the extended hand. "Jerry Parson. Live up the road. Me and the boys," he motioned to the dogs, "take a walk this way every-so-often. The boys were sniffin' and scratchin' at the door. I called out to Jessica and Mitch. No one replied, so I walked in." He looked the other way. "Wish I'd just called and not walked in."

"What's the last name of Jessica and Mitch?" Ryan pulled his notepad out.

"Told your buddy. Woodcock. Mitch's truck is gone. He must have the kids."

Ryan stared at the man. "Kids?"

"Jayden and Mia, twins. Think they're around seven." He glanced at the house then back at Ryan. "Glad those two weren't here."

Ryan pushed all this information around in his mind. Twins. Boy and girl. Was this what Shandra dreamed about? "Thank you. Did you give Deputy Speaks your information in case we have more questions?"

"I did. Can me and the boys go now?" The man's feet shifted back and forth.

"Yes. Thank you for hanging around." Ryan headed to the small one-story house. His first impression stepping through the open door was how could anyone raise two children in this mess. There were toys, piles of clothing, half-eaten food, and magazines, mostly entertainment, strewn about the living room.

"Speaks, where are you?" Ryan called out.

"Bedroom."

Ryan took several photos of the room, wondering if this was how they lived or if it had been tossed. He also wondered where the husband and children were. The kitchen was to the right of the living room. Bowls of soggy cereal, floating in milk, stood on the small table. Burnt toast stuck out of the toaster. There was a trail of mouse droppings across the floor. He shivered, not from fear of mice but the thought children lived in this mess.

He opened the first door he came to. The bathroom. Old fixtures and the avocado green bathtub dated the house. He backed out and tried the next door. The door opened halfway. It banged against a set of bunkbeds. A narrow dresser stood against the wall at the head of the bed. He shut the door and opened the last door.

The metallic smell of blood mixed with body excretions met his nostrils as his gaze landed on the thin, rigid female body dressed in jeans and t-shirt, bare feet. Dried blood made a path from her wrists to dark spots on the blanket under her hands. Her open eyes were blank, her mouth open, and jaw locked. A damp spot on the bed by her head drew Ryan's attention.

"Looks like suicide to me," Speaks said. He stood by the open window.

Ryan started at the door, taking photos of the scene. "I wouldn't be too certain. That doesn't look like deep enough cuts or enough blood for her to have died from blood loss." Moving further and further into the room, he continued taking photos until he was taking closeup shots of the cuts on her hands and then all angles up close to her face. He made sure the wet spot by her head was in a photo.

"Where are you?" called out Farley Smith, one of the Warner EMTs.

Speaks stepped out of the room.

Ryan heard low voices speaking before Dr. Roswell entered the room.

"Heard it's a suicide," the short, round man with thick glasses said, walking up to the bed.

"Don't put that on the death certificate just yet,

Doc," Ryan said, stepping back to let the man get a good look at the body.

After what seemed like half an hour, but in reality, about fifteen minutes, Dr. Roswell nodded. "Treat this like a homicide. There isn't enough blood, and she shows signs that could be poisoning. Won't know for sure until the autopsy. I'll recommend a full tox screening."

Ryan nodded.

The doctor filled out a piece of paper and handed it to Farley as the two met at the door to the room.

"Are you finished?" Farley asked.

"Not quite. I want to take a few more photos of the body as it is, then you can take it."

"Jessica Snyder, well, Woodcock since she married Mitch." Farley leaned against the door.

Ryan glanced over as the man flicked a tear off his cheek. He walked over to the EMT. "You knew her?"

"Yeah. We had several classes together in high school. Same grade until she dropped out. She was nice to everyone. But she tried too hard to make people like her." He shook his head. "When she married the star football player, and all the other girls were jealous, I thought she'd finally find happiness." He waved a hand toward the bed. "Never thought she'd do something like this."

Ryan decided not to let him know it was probably a homicide, not a suicide. Best to keep the killer unaware of what they knew by letting everyone believe the victim took her own life. "Any idea where the star football player is?"

"He works at Webb Automotive Repair in Huckleberry." His eyes widened. "Jesus, where are the kids?"

"Would they maybe be with a relative or friend?" Ryan hoped he'd find the two somewhere safe with family.

"She didn't have many friends. Family, you could try her sister, Andie Teague, but I doubt she'd have the kids. I heard she had a miscarriage not long ago and wasn't doing too well."

Ryan wrote down the sister's name. "What about grandparents?"

Farley shook his head. "Jessica's dad was in prison last I knew and her mom overdosed years ago. Mitch's parents haven't come back from Arizona. They usually stay there until the first of May."

"You can take her to the forensic lab in Coeur d'Alene." Ryan walked out of the room as the other EMT walked in.

Outside, he slipped into his vehicle and radioed dispatch. Cathleen, his older sister, answered. She worked days for the Weippe County Sheriff's Department.

"Ryan, heard you caught a suicide," she answered.

"Maybe not. Can you get me the phone number and address of Andie Teague, unsure of the town, and Webb Automotive Repair in Huckleberry?" He hoped the children were with the aunt or the dad took the day off and they were with him.

"Not a suicide? Sure. I'll text you the information you requested."

"Copy."

He stepped out of his vehicle as the EMTs rolled the gurney with the body bag out of the house.

Speaks walked over to him. "What do you want me

to do? There aren't any close neighbors to ask if they saw anything."

"Go talk to all of them up and down this road. Find out all you can about the family and when was the last time they saw Mitch Woodcock or the kids."

Ryan walked back into the house and began bagging everything that might be evidence. The first thing to go in the brown evidence bag was the single edged blade he'd found kicked under the bed. No matter how many times he dropped it from about where the woman's hand closest to the edge of the bed had been, the blade didn't bounce under the bed. Someone else had either cut her wrists and tossed or kicked the blade under the bed or after she'd cut herself, they'd knocked the blade to the floor and kicked it. Either way, this was looking more and more like murder. But what he didn't understand was what killed her? It was evident by the lack of blood that it had to be something other than the slit wrists.

Chapter Three

Shandra stood with one hand on Sheba's head and the other holding Apple's reins. She was glad her mare always had a level head. It was rare anything spooked or upset her.

Arnold had dug the hole where Lil had marked and was now lowering Sunshine into the earth. Once the horse's body was set, he began shoving dirt over the top. There was still some snow at this level of the mountain.

She was glad she'd worn her heavier coat and flannel-lined jeans. Shandra caught Arnold's attention.

He stopped the backhoe and opened the door. "Yeah?"

"When you're done, go back down the way we came up and leave the bill at the front door. I'll pay you when I come to town tomorrow." She waited for him to nod in agreement before swinging up in the saddle and heading around the mountain.

As they'd stood here, she'd remembered there was a ledge, similar to the one she'd seen in her dream, on the neighbor's property to the east of her. The Flanders had given her an open invitation to ride on their land whenever she wanted. She thought maybe they hoped she'd find a good clay source and they could charge her for the mud and say they provided the material for her vases.

The clay source she'd found on her property would keep her in material until she was too old to work a pottery wheel.

Sheba walked ahead of the horse, her fluffy tail waving.

Shandra breathed in the crisp air, pungent pine, and mustiness of the wet ground Apple's hooves disturbed. This was her favorite place and her favorite thing to do. Horseback riding on Huckleberry Mountain. Her happiest moments as a child were when she rode a horse around her stepfather's Montana ranch. Now, she loved when Ryan rode on the mountain with her. She loved sharing the rhythm of the horses, the smells, and the muffled steps and singing birds. This was heaven to her.

Sheba let out a soft woof and took off loping through the trees.

"Wait for me," Shandra said, urging Apple into an extended trot to keep the dog in sight and yet slow enough she could see any branches that might catch her off guard.

She wove in and out of trees, ducking limbs. Sheba stopped at the base of the ledge she'd been aiming for.

Peering up the side of the cliff, Shandra focused on the ledge but didn't see anything.

"Hello?" she called.

Sheba walked back to her and the horse and sat, staring up at her.

"Well, you brought me here. Wasn't it because you knew we'd find two children?" Shandra studied her dog.

Sheba stared back and wagged her tail.

"Then what did you hear?"

The thud of small hooves striking rock, echoed above her. A glance at the ledge revealed a buck standing on the outcropping as if he were a king getting ready to give a speech to his kingdom.

"We followed him?" she asked Sheba.

The buck snorted and spun, disappearing.

"Well, we checked out the ledge." On one hand she was happy they didn't find any scared children and on the other hand, she worried about the two and wondered where they were and if they were safe.

~*~

After discovering the victim's sister lived in Warner and the victim's husband worked in Huckleberry, Ryan called Webb Automotive Repair to see if the victim's husband was there.

"Haven't seen Mitch since Friday," the owner, Richard Webb said.

"Was he supposed to come into work today?" Ryan asked.

"No. I fired him last Friday." Mr. Webb said it as if he didn't care about the Woodcock family.

"Why did you fire him?" Ryan wondered if being fired had caused the man to do something to make less mouths to feed. He hoped the children were still safe.

"I had my reasons. Why are you asking all of these

questions?" The man sounded leery.

"Jessica Woodcock's body was found this morning by a neighbor. I'm trying to contact her husband."

"Jesus. What happened to her?" This was the first show of sympathy he'd heard in the man's tone.

"I can't say at this time. You wouldn't happen to know where Mitch or the kids might be?"

"The kids weren't with her? Thank God. Those two are the only good thing that came out of that marriage." Affection warmed Webb's voice.

"Where do you think I might find Mitch?" Ryan asked, again.

"His folks are gone until May. You might try their house, or I think he has a cabin on Huckleberry somewhere." There was a pause. "Did you check with the school to see if the kids are there?"

"Which school?"

"Huckleberry Elementary. I think their teacher is Mrs. Couch."

"Thank you. If you hear from Mitch, have him give me a call." Ryan rattled off his phone number and immediately dialed the school.

"Huckleberry Elementary, this is Leah, how may I help you?" answered a young woman.

"I'm Weippe County Detective Greer. Could you tell me if Jayden and Mia Woodcock are in class today?"

The woman sucked in air. "Is everything okay?"

"Are they there?" he asked.

"Let me check Mrs. Couch's roster for this morning. Please hold while I check."

"Thank you." In the silence, he hoped the two were safe in a classroom.

"Detective, they are marked absent on the roster. Is there a problem?"

"I'm not at liberty to say. Thank you for your help." He disconnected. "Damn!" If Shandra hadn't dreamed about two children fitting the Woodcock's description, he wouldn't be so worried about them. But he believed in her dreams, and he had a suspicion they were going to have to call out the search and rescue to look for the children.

Ryan touched the number Cathleen had sent him for Andie, Jessica's sister, and waited while the phone rang.

"Hello?" the woman's voice answered with caution.

"Andie Teague?" Ryan asked.

"Yes. Who are you?" The accusation in the woman's tone had Ryan wondering what the woman was worried about.

"Weippe County Detective Greer. Ma'am, do you have Jayden and Mia Woodcock with you?"

"Jayden and Mia? No. Why are you asking? Did something happen to Jessica and Mitch? Was it a car accident? I told those two to get a better vehicle. What they had wasn't safe for hauling around kids."

"I'm sorry, your sister is dead. We found her body at her house this morning. We can't find Mitch or the kids. Do you have any idea where they might be?" Ryan was glad the aunt was concerned about the children.

"It's Monday, the kids should be in school and Mitch at work."

"The children aren't in school. Mitch was fired last Friday."

"Oh no! Did he kill Jessica and run off with the kids? How dare he take my niece and nephew away from me. I've had enough loss." Sobbing noises came from the phone.

"Mrs. Teague, please. Could you hold it together to help me figure out where Mitch and the children might be?" Ryan wished he was at the woman's house to see if the tears were real or fake.

Sniffing, and then, "Yes, yes. That's what is important. Little Jayden and Mia. Mitch's parents have a house toward Hafersville. And I think he and Jessica had a cabin out that way too. I can go look—"

"No. It would be best if you stay home. That way we'll know where to contact you when we find the children," Ryan hastily said. He didn't need this woman getting in the middle of his homicide investigation. He already had his wife in the middle of it.

Chapter Four

Arriving back at her barn, Shandra saw Lil's pickup hadn't returned. It meant her friend was either still in town or headed home. Her stomach growled. It was two hours after lunchtime. No wonder her stomach was protesting.

She put Apple in the corral with the other horses and headed to the house to make a sandwich. Sheba bounded out of the forest forty feet from the back of the house.

"Where have you been?" Shandra scratched the dog's ears and opened the back door.

Her phone rang as she entered the house. She'd left it behind when Arnold showed up to take care of Sunshine.

The *Dream a Little Dream* tune was winding down, when she picked up the phone and answered. "Hello?"

"Did you get Sunshine buried?" Lil asked.

"Yes. She should be happy there." Shandra wasn't sure how long it would take her feisty friend to get over the loss.

"Good. Claude invited me to dinner. I won't be home until after dark."

"Thank you for letting me know." Shandra smiled. After all the years of Claude liking Lil, he had finally found the nerve to talk to her about something other than what kind of feed to buy.

The call disconnected.

Lil was a woman of few words.

Shandra's stomach growled. In the kitchen, she pulled out all the ingredients to make a deli style turkey sandwich and began layering the mayonnaise, mustard, relish, lettuce, tomato, cheese, and turkey. She put the top slice of bread on the tower of food as her phone beeped.

Ryan.

She checked the text message.

I'll be late tonight. Caught a homicide.

Her chest squeezed. *Was it 2 children?*

No.

She sucked in a deep breath, realizing she'd been holding it. *Thank goodness!*

The woman had 2 children who fit the two in your dream.

Before she could text anything, he added- *And we don't know where they are.*

Do you want me to help look for them?

No. I'll tell you more when I get home if you're still up.

Ok.

She wasn't hungry anymore. Shandra packed the plate with the sandwich into the great room and placed it on the coffee table. She lay down on the couch and closed her eyes. "Ella come to me and help these children," she whispered and allowed her body to relax and quieted her mind.

~*~

Deputy Trapp met Ryan at the Woodcock cabin about 5 miles from Mitch's parents' place, which he'd found vacant fifteen minutes earlier. Mitch's extended cab, 1988 Ford pickup was parked in front of the cabin.

Ryan hoped that meant the man and children were inside. He walked up to the door and knocked.

"Mitch Woodcock, this is the Weippe County Sheriff's Department. We'd like to have a word with you." He waited. There wasn't a sound coming from inside. "Go around back and check things out." He waved Deputy Trapp to the left of the cabin.

Ryan knocked one more time and called out. Still nothing. He tried the door knob. It turned. Pushing the door open slowly, he held his Glock in one hand as he entered. The building was dark, but the smell told him he wasn't going to like what he found.

~*~

Two children huddled together. One was crying as Shandra and Ella sat in a tree staring down at them. "Grandmother, we have to go to them." Shandra started to climb down from the tree, but Ella put a hand on her arm, gathering her attention. "What?"

Grandmother swept her arm in a slow arc as if showing off the forest with a flourish. That's when she understood. Study the area. Figure out where the children are. Shandra's gaze took in the arc her grandmother's arm had made. There weren't just pine and fir trees, there were aspen and alder. More of the leafy trees than the evergreens. The rocks weren't the type found on her property on Huckleberry. And the ground was flat. The children weren't on a mountainside.

Just as she started to climb down the tree to go to the children, the scene disappeared.

A loud burp awakened Shandra from her light sleep. She opened her eyes and found Sheba sitting at the end of the coffee table, her wide pink tongue slid along each side of her mouth. The sandwich that had been on the plate… gone.

"You ate my lunch!" Shandra said, sitting up.

Sheba's ears drooped, and she slowly walked over to the rug in front of the fireplace.

Shandra wandered into the kitchen with the empty plate and grabbed an apple. "I'm going to Ruthie's for a burger. There aren't any dogs there to eat my…" She glanced at the kitchen clock, a horse head with eyes and a tail that moved back and forth ticking off the seconds. "Dinner."

She walked out to the corral, fed the horses, and drove her Jeep out of the barn, closing the doors behind her. Maybe she could catch up to Ryan and have dinner with him.

A quick text, *I'm headed to Ruthie's for dinner,* and she headed down her driveway to the county road.

~*~

Ryan leaned against the outside of the cabin waiting for Dr. Porter and Maxwell Treat. Dr. Porter, Alex, as they'd started calling him since Shandra's friend Miranda married him, was the closest medical examiner since he lived and worked in Huckleberry. Maxwell Treat was married to Shandra's best friend, Ruthie, who owned Ruthie's Diner in Huckleberry.

He received a text.

Shandra. *I'm headed to Ruthie's for dinner.*

Ryan glanced at the time. It was early for dinner but the burying of Lil's horse could have taken longer than Shandra had expected. He texted back, *Enjoy.*

There wasn't any way he was going to tell her the father of the two children was also dead. She'd move heaven and earth to find the children if she knew they were lost and the parents were dead.

The good thing about this homicide, it was clearly a death by another person. The man had a shotgun blast to the torso. The mess a shotgun makes was never something Ryan liked to dig around in. But it was his job to take photos and look for evidence. They didn't have a forensic team to come in and search the cabin. It was up to him and Deputy Trapp to discover all the evidence.

There was a shotgun hanging on a rack above the door. He'd bagged it as evidence. It had smelled as if it had been shot recently. The way it had been hung back up, if it was the murder weapon, he was pretty sure any prints had been wiped off. Trapp also found a shell casing behind the door.

What he found particularly interesting; the husband had been killed before the wife. Which made him wonder if he had misjudged the suicide. Could the woman have killed her husband then in remorse, killed herself?

The Treat Mortuary pick-up van arrived. Alex sat in the passenger seat. Maxwell must have swung by the clinic and picked the doctor up. The van pulled up close to the front of the cabin.

"Doesn't this belong to Mitch Woodcock?" Maxwell asked, straightening out of the van. He was well over six feet, shoulders broad enough to be a pro football player. His brown skin and stature were a striking contrast to Alex's albino features, average height, and slender build.

"Yes. It's his body." Ryan led the way into the two-room cabin. An open living space and one bedroom. No running water and an outhouse behind.

"Man, does Jessica know yet?" Maxwell asked.

Ryan stopped and studied his friend. "I found her body this morning."

Maxwell said several words that made Alex cringe. "What about the kids? They had twins."

"I haven't been able to find them." Ryan waved to the bloody body sprawled in a wooden chair.

Alex walked up to the body and studied it with more interest than he had when he first became a medical examiner. It seemed he no longer took this job for granted and actually cared what had happened to the victims.

"Definitely killed by a round from a shotgun," Alex stated matter-of-factly. "I'd say the person who shot him was standing by the door. See the size of the hole?" He pointed at the entry wound. "If the shooter had been closer there would have been gunpowder and possible stippling on the skin."

"Thanks, Alex." Ryan added that observation to his notepad and measured the distance from the door to the body, adding that information as well.

Maxwell kept talking, whether to himself or for

them to hear, as he put the victim in a body bag. "I don't understand. Who would want to kill Jessica and Mitch? It's been eight years since she stole him from anyone. That would be a long time to carry a jealousy. And why both of them? Doesn't make any sense." Maxwell stopped muttering and asked Alex, "Want to help me lift him onto the gurney?"

The doctor nodded, and they settled the body bag on the gurney and wheeled it out. Ryan went to work looking for any evidence that might have been under the body.

Deputy Trapp returned. "I found two sets of small footprints about fifty yards up in the forest. Looks like they were wandering around and then larger prints joined them, and they walked back down to the county road."

"We need to find out if the Woodcocks had two vehicles. Then we need to canvas the area and see if anyone saw an adult with these two." Ryan picked up a stick frame with a photo of the family. He pulled the photo off and handed it to Trapp. "Ask every household up and down this road. We have to find those two kids."

Chapter Five

Ruthie's Diner was bustling with activity when
Shandra walked in. She enjoyed the new '50s décor that
had been incorporated when an arsonist tried to burn
the place down over two years ago.

"Only one?" Ruthie asked, carrying Donnie on her
back in a baby pack.

"Ryan's working." She tickled the nearly one-year-
old under the chin when his mother spun for Shandra to
say hi.

"Maxwell said he'd be late coming home. There
was a murder out past your house." Ruthie was facing
her now.

"Past my house? Then there were two today." A
shiver crawled up her spine.

"Two? Maxwell only had the one body to pick up."
Ruthie studied her.

"There was one toward Warner this morning. Why didn't Ryan tell me there was another dead person?" She said it more for her own sake than expecting an answer from her friend.

"Maybe because his job isn't all ice cream and roses. What'll you have?" Ruthie asked, her order book in her hand.

"I need cheered up. I'll have a caramel shake first and then you can bring me a cheeseburger and sweet potato fries." She tugged on one of Donnie's feet dangling at Ruthie's side.

"I'll get the shake right out and get Uncle Orin making your burger and fries." Ruthie spun to head to the kitchen and Shandra waved at Donnie.

She was happy for her friend. Ruthie and Maxwell had dated for years and now they were married with a cute little boy. She sighed. Even Miranda was glowing these days. She and Alex were expecting their first child. The last time they'd talked, her friend had been animated about the progress Alex was making on discovering a cure for the hereditary disease that had killed his father and grandfather in their fifties.

Fifty was coming up for the doctor. Shandra would turn forty this year. Ryan was forty-one. They'd been discussing the things that could go wrong with her having children at her age. They'd had over a year of marriage, just the two of them. They were ready to add to the family. They just weren't sure how.

The vision of the two children from her dream flashed. Could they be the answer to her question? But how? Both parents would have to be… The shiver crept up her spine, again. Was the second body the father?

Ruthie arrived with the shake. This time she carried

Donnie in her arms and sat on the bench across the table from Shandra. She slid the shake and a straw across the table. "What's going on? You look like you haven't slept?"

She should have known her best friend would notice she wasn't her usual self. "I didn't sleep well last night. Then Lil's horse, Sunshine, died during the night. She couldn't handle the burial. I tended to that most of the day." She slurped a mouthful of cold, sweet, caramel goodness.

"Oh no! Is Lil doing alright?"

"She's having dinner with Claude." That put a smile on Shandra's face. "I think the two of them are getting along very well."

Ruthie snickered. "Claude has been sweet on her for a long time. I can't believe it took Lil this long to pick up on it."

"I'm happy she finally found someone who makes her look forward to the next day." She used the spoon to serve Donnie a small sip of her shake.

"What about you? Is Ryan enough to make you look forward to the next day?"

Shandra peered at her friend. "Yes. He is. But what you're really asking is, have we started working on a family. The answer is, we're still discussing."

"What's to discuss? You turn forty this year. After that the chances of you having complications or the child having difficulties is higher each year. You should be grabbing that man every chance you get and hauling him to the bedroom."

Shandra laughed. "Is that how you and Maxwell got Donnie?"

Ruthie's mahogany cheeks darkened. "No. Turns

out, I'm just very fertile."

"I'm happy for the two of you and Alex and Miranda. But Ryan and I are thinking about going a different direction." She slipped her mouth over the straw and sipped her shake.

"Order up!" Orin called out.

Ruthie slid off of the bench. "I'm interested in hearing more." She walked to retrieve the food and Shandra pulled out her phone.

Is the body you're with now the father of the children?

~*~

Ryan felt the buzz of his phone as he pulled in their driveway. It was closer for him to pull in and grab a sandwich at home than drive to Huckleberry and wait for someone to make something. It would be even quicker because Shandra wasn't home.

Parking in front of the house, he glanced at his phone. "How did she find out?"

He entered the house, and Sheba bounded out the open door. "Don't go very far, I have to get going," he called to the dog and walked into the kitchen.

Pulling out ingredients to make a sandwich, he dialed Shandra.

"Is the body you are investigating now the father of the two children?" she asked in an accusing tone.

He sighed. "Yes. I didn't want to tell you, so you wouldn't get yourself in trouble."

"Where are you?"

"Home. Making a sandwich." He layered the ingredients for a turkey sandwich and slapped a slice of bread on top.

"I could have had that ready for you if I hadn't

decided to come to town. I didn't like sitting at home all by myself."

"That doesn't usually bother you," he said, taking a bite and heading for the door.

"I had another dream. I know where the children are."

He stopped at the open back door. "Where?"

"I don't know exactly. I'll know it when I see it. But it's flat with aspen trees and pine and the rocks are like river rock, not granite and slate like is on the mountain."

What she explained sounded like the area around the Woodcock house between Huckleberry and Warner. "Where are you?"

"Ruthie's."

"Stay there. I'll come pick you up." He ended the connection and whistled for Sheba. It was almost dark. He should wait to take Shandra to the area in the morning, but if the two children were out overnight and not dressed properly, they could get hypothermia and possibly die.

Sheba bounded into the house, Ryan closed the door, finished the sandwich in three bites, and slid into his SUV. He hoped they had luck finding the children. If they were roaming around near their house, there was a good chance they knew who killed their mother.

Chapter Six

The vehicle's headlights flashed across a small one-story house. Shandra stared at the home for a moment before concentrating on the trees behind. "These look like the kind of trees in my dream."

The crime scene tape across the door of the house had her chest squeezing. They had to find the two children.

"I'm surprised there isn't anyone from search and rescue here," Shandra said, slipping out of Ryan's work vehicle.

"The tracks at the cabin indicated the children are with someone. I couldn't call out search and rescue to look here because you had a dream."

The frustration in Ryan's voice told her he was as worried about the children as she was.

"Do you think the mom killed the dad and brought the children here? That maybe they saw who killed her?" Shandra's heart raced. What might the two have seen?

"That's what Oldham thinks. But I'm still sure the forensic lab will discover she didn't die from the slits on her wrist. They weren't deep enough and there wasn't enough blood." He handed her a long, heavy flashlight like the ones she'd witness search and rescue members use. "Let's see if we can find any footprints."

"I wish we had Sheba. She'd sniff them out." Shandra knew her big mutt was scared of her own shadow, but for some reason children loved her and she loved children.

"She'd be hiding behind us." Ryan followed a narrow dirt path to the back of the house. "I hope Speaks didn't cover up any tracks when he came around this morning."

Shandra stood behind Ryan while he scanned the ground with the beam of his flashlight. "What about the neighbor who found her? Do you think he'd be willing to help look for the children?"

Ryan faced her. "He seemed to care about the two. And he has two dogs that might know the kids. But what do we tell him when he asks why we didn't call out search and rescue?"

She shrugged. "That you couldn't find them anywhere else and have a hunch they might be here." She smiled as the edge of his flashlight beam lit her face.

His chuckle and the sound of him taking his phone out of his belt holster broadened her smile.

"Hello, Mr. Parson, this is Detective Greer, we spoke this morning at the Woodcock place. We found Mr. Woodcock. I'm afraid he's deceased." A pause. "No, he didn't take his own life. But I can't find the children. I wondered if you and your dogs could head through the forest from your place toward the Woodcock residence." A pause. "Yes, I have reason to believe they might be somewhere out in the woods. Thank you." Ryan returned to looking at the ground.

"Is he coming?" Shandra asked, knowing he must be for Ryan to have thanked the man.

"Yes. He said if he'd thought the kids were out in the woods, he and the dogs would have been looking for them all day." Ryan pointed. "Two sets of small footprints." He held his hand toward her.

Grasping Ryan's hand, she followed him deeper into the trees. After about twenty minutes, Shandra asked. "Should we call their names?"

"They don't know us. They may try to hide if we call out to them. The trail is easy to follow. Let's stick to following it." Ryan squeezed her hand.

Ten minutes later a booming voice could be heard. "Jayden, Mia, it's Jerry, Pike, and Rambo. Come on out."

Ryan continued the way he was going.

"Shouldn't we go toward the neighbor?" Shandra asked.

"I'm going to stick with the facts. The footprints." Ryan swept the beam of light from left to right.

Shandra gripped his hand tight. "Swing your light back to the right." She was sure a rock like she'd seen in her dream had been in the beam of light.

The light moved to the right and there was the rock. Shandra walked into the beam, moving toward the smooth round boulder. "Jayden? Mia? I'm a friend. I'm here to take you someplace warm and make you hot chocolate," she said in a normal voice.

"With marshmallows?" a little girl's voice asked.

Shandra's heart warmed. "Yes, with marshmallows. Come on out. You're safe with us."

A child with shoulder length hair in knots with bits of twigs and leaves sticking out of it, walked out from behind the boulder. She looked like a wood nymph. Her big eyes stared at Shandra. Her clothes were dirty.

"Come on," the child said to the back side of the boulder and a male version of her stepped into the beam of the light.

Shandra knew she was a stranger to the two children, so she held back hugging them like she wanted to. "I'm Shandra. This is my husband, Ryan. He's a policeman. We've been looking for you."

Barking and snarling came from their right. Shandra spun toward the sound as two dark creatures raced toward them.

"Pike, Rambo, no!" the girl shouted.

The two dogs stopped as if they'd run into a wall of glass and plopped onto their bottoms.

"Mr. Parson and his dogs were helping us look for you," Ryan said, walking up beside Shandra. She glanced over her shoulder at him. He was slipping his weapon back into his holster. He'd been going to shoot the dogs. She was glad the animals had listened to the child. She didn't want them to have seen the dogs get shot. Not if they had already witnessed their mother's death that morning.

Crashing of brush caused the two animals to spin and run toward the sound.

"Mr. Parson! We're over here. We found them!" Ryan called.

Shandra walked up to the children and held out a hand to each of them. "How about we go to our house for that hot chocolate, a bath, and a warm bed?"

The neighbor arrived with the dogs on his heels. "Jayden, Mia, thank God, we found you." He stopped about ten feet back from all of them. "Why'd you hide out back here?"

Ryan cut into the man's questions. "Thank you for your help. We have them and will get them cared for." He walked away from Shandra and the children to speak to the man alone.

Mr. Parson glanced over Ryan's shoulder at the kids and stopped about thirty feet away. "Where you taking them?"

"For tonight, our house. There's no sense in upsetting them more by calling in children's services. And I want to see if they know anything about either of their parent's deaths." Ryan slapped the man on the back. "Thanks for coming out and helping."

"I wasn't much help. Looked like you and that woman found them just fine." He narrowed his gaze. "She another cop?"

"She's my wife." Pride filled his words. Ryan was so glad fate had brought him and Shandra together several years ago, even if she had been the prime suspect in a murder investigation.

Parson whistled to the dogs. They trotted toward him. "Let me know where the two end up."

"I will. And I'll be back with some more questions in the next couple of days." Ryan headed back to the trio standing in the light of Shandra's flashlight.

"Let's go." Ryan didn't miss the joy on Shandra's face as she led the two children back the way they'd come. Fifteen minutes and it was evident the two were too tired to walk the rest of the way.

"Come on." He picked up Jayden in one arm, handed his flashlight to Shandra and picked up Mia in his other arm. The girl put her arms around his neck and his insides did a strange flip.

Shandra's eyes sparkled when she smiled at him before taking the lead and shining the light for him to see.

At the SUV, he buckled them in the back seat, still sleeping, and took his place behind the steering wheel.

"Do you need to call in that you found them?" Shandra whispered.

"I'll call in the morning. Let's get them fed, cleaned up, and in bed."

She smiled. "I'll call Lil and ask her to make grilled cheese sandwiches and hot chocolate."

Just as they entered Huckleberry, Jayden started fussing in his sleep. "Don't hurt her, don't!" he murmured.

Ryan nodded for Shandra to wake the child up. No sense in him having bad dreams.

"Jayden, it's me, Shandra. Wake up. Think of happy things," Shandra leaned between the two front seats.

Ryan drove slower than normal. He had not only his wife in his vehicle, but two children who had gone through enough grief.

"Where are we going?" the young boy asked.

"To our house for the night. Tomorrow, we'll see what happens." Shandra replied.

While her words sounded upbeat, he heard the undertone of worry.

"I want Momma and Daddy." Jayden's tone was combative.

"They aren't here. We'll take care of you," Shandra said.

Ryan had a feeling he'd be calling his sisters for advice on how to deal with the two children. He needed to know if they saw anything, who brought them from the cabin back to their house, and if they saw their mother dying.

Chapter Seven

Lil and Sheba met them at the back door. Shandra led Mia into the house, holding the child's small hand.

"You have a castle!" the girl exclaimed.

Shandra laughed. "It doesn't look like one, but it feels like a castle to me."

"And a dog!"

Sheba rested her head on the girl's shoulder. Mia ruffled the long hair on the dog's neck.

Jayden walked over and hugged Sheba around the neck.

Shandra filled with pride that her dog could help the children show their loss. Tears glistened in their eyes.

"I didn't make these grilled cheese sandwiches to let them get cold," Lil said, but without the same acidic lilt as usual.

The two released Sheba.

"You can wash your hands in there," Shandra pointed to the hall bathroom.

The two walked in the room. She stood by the door watching as they used the soap and washed their dirty hands until they were clean.

"Come on." Shandra herded them into the kitchen.

"I didn't know how many marshmallows you liked so I put them in a bowl," Lil said. Her cheeks turned red as Shandra mouthed 'thank you.'

"I got everything done you asked. I'm goin' to bed." Lil stormed out of the kitchen, and the back door closed with more force than was necessary.

"Why's she mad?" Mia asked.

"Because she doesn't like people to know she has a heart," Ryan said, picking up half of one of the sandwiches on the plate.

"Everyone has a heart," Jayden said, staring at Ryan as if he were trying to decide if the man wasn't smart enough to know that.

"Yes, they do. Lil can be gruff, but it's because she didn't grow up with as much love as most people, so she doesn't know how to show it sometimes and it embarrasses her." Shandra motioned for the children to grab a sandwich.

"She was a sad little girl?" Mia asked, sitting with her hands in her lap.

"Yes, until her grandparents took her in." Shandra only knew a few pieces of Lil's life. The little bits she'd been willing to share over the years.

Mia looked up at Shandra with tears in her eyes. "I don't want to live with Grandma and Grandpa. They don't let us eat in the living room."

Shandra put an arm around the little girl's

shoulders. "But they are family. We'll have to see what happens. For now, you two need to eat, get baths, and a good night's sleep. If you think you'll be scared during the night, I'm pretty sure we can persuade a big fluffy dog to sleep in your room." She tipped her head toward Sheba, sitting between the two. Drool dangled from her mouth, anticipating dropped food. The dog had quickly learned when Ryan's nieces and nephews were around there were tidbits that could be gobbled up off the floor.

"Really, the dog can sleep with us?" Mia picked up half a sandwich and started chewing.

"Her name is Sheba."

The dog woofed and peered at first the girl and then the boy with sad eyes.

"Sheba." Jayden patted the big furry head.

~*~

The children were in bed, with Sheba laying in the middle of the queen-sized bed between them.

Shandra sat on the couch sipping chamomile tea and waiting for Ryan to finish his shower. She knew he would have to call and let children's services know they'd found the children, but she didn't want them to leave. In just the few short hours they'd been in her life, she felt the last chink in her heart fill.

With the childhood she'd had after her father died, and the one bad relationship in college, she hadn't planned on marrying or having children. Ryan changed the marrying idea. She smiled. He'd believed in her before she'd believed in herself. He'd shown her unconditional love. Something she hadn't received until she'd reunited with her Nez Perce family.

She and Ryan had talked about having children, but worried with his job, that she might end up raising them alone. She would never remarry and thrust a stepfather on them. She closed her eyes and swallowed the hatred that reared in her mind and in her heart when thinking of the man who took her father's life and then took her heritage from her.

"Hey, that's a pretty stormy face for having two children under your roof." Ryan walked into the great room dressed in a t-shirt and flannel pajama bottoms.

"My thoughts started out rainbows and puppy dog tails and ended up on Adam."

Ryan plopped on the couch beside her and put an arm around her. "He's gone. You've picked up the pieces and have a wonderful life." He kissed her. "And for the night, have two precocious children under your roof."

She faced him. "Do we have to turn them over to Children's Services tomorrow?"

Ryan studied his wife. She had become attached to the brother and sister. He'd felt it the moment she'd found them behind the boulder. "I'll talk to them in the morning. See if they saw or heard anything that can help us discover who killed their parents. I didn't want to press them tonight. They'd been through enough. I should have the forensic report in the morning and know exactly when their father was killed and possibly know if the mother committed suicide or had help."

"When do you have to tell someone you have the children?" She slid down on the couch and leaned her head on his chest.

"I'll call Oldham in the morning and let him know we have them and ask him to hold off saying anything to anyone other than their family until I figure out if the kids know anything. They feel safe here. We're more likely to get them to talk here than taking them to the station."

"I agree." She glanced toward the hall and the guest bedroom. "I think I'll sleep on the couch tonight so I can hear them if they wake up and are disoriented."

"Then I guess, I'll turn out the light and join you."

~*~

A noise roused Shandra. She sat up and remembered they slept on the couch. There it was again. Almost a whimper but not like the sound Sheba made.

She tip-toed across the room and down the hall to the guest bedroom. The light they'd left on in the kitchen shone enough into the room that she could see Jayden was hugging Sheba, who licked his arm. The whimpering came from the boy.

Shandra sat down on the side of the bed and put a hand on his back, rubbing in a circle. "Shhh. You're safe now. Go back to sleep." She continued rubbing his back until he released the dog and relaxed onto the pillow.

Mia was sound asleep, but her face was scrunched as if she were in pain.

Shandra's heart went out to the twins. She knew the pain of losing a beloved parent. What must it feel like to lose both of them? And feel your grandparents didn't want you? That's how she felt as a child. Her mother and stepfather told her her father's family didn't want to see her. Her maternal grandmother had left her money but had rarely visited or asked for her to visit.

She wondered about Jessica's parents. Were those the ones Mia had commented about or had it been Mitch's parents?

Patting Sheba on the head, she rose off the bed. "Good girl. You finally found your calling," Shandra whispered and stood.

The cowardly dog had found someone to help that didn't require her to face anything other than unseen nightmares or scary thoughts.

Chapter Eight

Running feet and the clack of nails on the wood floor woke Shandra. Opening her eyes, sunshine shone through the windows. She shoved the blankets over her, down to her feet and sniffed.

Cinnamon! Ryan must have pulled a pan of her cinnamon rolls out of the freezer and put them in the oven.

Sheba charged out of the kitchen and over to the sofa. Her eyes were lit with excitement. It appeared her dog enjoyed having the children to play with.

"What did you do with Jayden and Mia?" Shandra asked, patting her dog's head.

"We're here!" shouted Mia, running across the room from the kitchen. Jayden appeared not as enthusiastically from the hall.

"If you are here, who is making the house smell so yummy?" Shandra asked.

"Ryan!" Mia tugged on Shandra's hand. "He said

to wake up the sleepy head so we could eat."

"He called me a sleepy head?" Shandra asked, rising off the couch and following the girl into the kitchen.

Mia nodded her head. "He did." The girl climbed up onto a stool.

Jayden walked into the room, broodier than he had been when they found him. Shandra studied the boy. He had a dullness to his gaze that made her wonder if he might have seen something that Mia hadn't.

Ryan deposited plates in front of them bearing a cinnamon roll and scrambled eggs with cheese.

"Our daddy never makes breakfast," Mia said, and she set the fork back down on the counter. "Can we see Mommy and Daddy today?"

Shandra's chest squeezed. It was apparent the child didn't understand her parents were gone.

"Stupid, I told you, they're dead. We won't ever see them again!" Jayden had been climbing up onto the stool. He jumped down and ran down the hall.

Shandra started to stand, but Ryan waved her to stay. He followed the boy out of the kitchen.

"What does Jayden mean we won't see them again?" Mia asked, her eyes filling with tears.

Shandra pulled the child onto her lap. "I'm afraid, he's right. Ryan is trying to find out what happened to your mommy and daddy. They are both dead. Do you know what that means?"

The girl nodded and sniffed. "Our dog, Pogo, died before Christmas. He didn't move. Wouldn't come when we called. Daddy dug a hole in the backyard and put him in, covering him with dirt." Her mouth twisted in horror. "Are Mommy and Daddy going to be put in the ground and covered up?"

Shandra hugged the child tight. "Shhh. We'll talk about that later." It was obvious to her, Mia hadn't seen anything but poor Jayden had. She hoped Ryan was able to get the boy to tell him what he'd seen.

~*~

Jayden lay across the bed on his belly. His face was buried in his crossed arms. The way his small body shook, Ryan could tell the boy was crying.

"Hey," Ryan lay down on the bed like the boy. He'd been a boy once and knew it was easier to talk to an adult when you weren't looking at them. "Since you know your parents are dead, I think you know what happened to them. Could you tell me, so we can put the person who killed them in jail?"

The boy sniffed, rubbed his nose back and forth on an arm, and hiccupped.

This might be harder than he thought. Either the boy was covering for someone, or he had been traumatized more than Ryan first believed.

He'd start with what he thought he knew. "Were you and your sister with your dad at the cabin over the weekend?"

"Mommy wasn't feeling good. She was like that sometimes. Daddy said we'd go to the cabin and go hiking." He rubbed his chin back and forth across his arm.

"You like to hike?" Ryan asked, hoping to get the boy to warm up to him.

"I do. Mia talks too much and scares the animals. Daddy didn't care, but I like to see the animals."

Ryan chuckled. "Yeah, some girls talk a lot."

Jayden rolled to his side, propping his head up with

one arm. "Does Shandra talk a lot?"

"No, that's one of the things I like about her. She knows when to be quiet."

Jayden smiled. "I like that, too."

It appeared his wife had made a huge impact on the boy in a few hours. "Was there anyone at the cabin with your dad and you?"

"Besides Mia?" The boy stared at the bedspread where he picked at a string.

"Yeah? I know someone took you back to your house. We saw the tracks."

"That was Mrs. Webb. She found us after Daddy told us to go for a walk." He closed his eyes tight then opened them and stared Ryan in the eyes. "When we were in the forest looking for pine cones, I heard a loud sound like a gun. I told Mia to keep looking for pine cones, I'd be back." He closed his eyes and tears trickled out at the corners. "I saw Daddy. Bloody. His eyes open."

Ryan put an arm around the boy. That was something he never wanted a child to see. "You knew he was dead," he whispered.

"Yeah. But I didn't tell Mia. I went back to her and tried to think what to do when Mrs. Webb called to us and said she'd take us home. She wouldn't look me in the eye. I knew she'd seen Daddy, too."

Ryan wondered how the woman knew the family was there and had the intuition to look for the kids?

"Did you say anything to Mrs. Webb?"

Jayden shook his head. "I didn't want Mia to know."

"Did she speak to your mom when she brought you home?" Ryan wondered what the mother would have thought about her husband's boss's wife bringing the children back from a weekend with their father.

"She dropped us off before we could see the house. She said our mom wouldn't want to see her." The boy sniffed. "Mia talked all the way home about why didn't she bring Daddy. Mrs. Webb made up all kinds of excuses."

Did the boy think Mrs. Webb had killed his father? If so, why hadn't he come out and said so?

"Did you tell your mom about your dad?"

His face puckered up and tears streamed down his face. "She told me I was a liar. Daddy wasn't dead. She didn't believe what I said because Mia said I was lying, too."

Now he understood the boy's hesitation to say anything.

"He is dead. I discovered his body after I found your mom." Ryan peered into the boy's eyes. "Do you know what happened to your mom?"

He shook his head. "She said she was going to call Aunt Andie and we were to go outside and play." He wiped a hand under his running nose.

"Did you see your aunt come? Did she look for you?" Ryan wondered why the woman had acted as if she didn't know anything about Mitch's death when her sister would have said something.

"I don't know. We went to play and it started getting dark. When we went back to the house, it was dark, Mommy was laying on her bed. She didn't say anything. We made cereal and went to bed."

"Was it in the morning, before Mr. Parson came by that you realized she was dead, too?" Ryan hated bringing all of this back up, but the boy was their only witness to both the deaths.

"I went into Mommy's room. She had her eyes open but she didn't say anything. She was cold, and I saw the blood. Like Daddy." His voice shook. "I put food in a backpack and told Mia we were going hiking. She's such a girl. She wanted to go to school. I told her it was a no school day."

Ryan held back a chuckle. "Did she believe you?"

"Not really, but she didn't want me hiking by myself. Daddy always told us to hike in pairs." His eyes teared up, again.

"Thank you for telling me all of this. It will help me find the person or persons responsible for hurting your parents." He patted the boy on the back. "Let's go get some breakfast. Your sister is going to need you to help her understand about your parents."

Jayden slid to the edge of the bed and stood. "It's hard being the oldest by an hour."

Chapter Nine

Shandra set the cup of hot chocolate she'd made for Jayden at his spot at the kitchen island when he and Ryan returned to the kitchen. From Ryan's furrowed brow and the boy's steady gaze on his sister, Jayden must have told Ryan what he knew.

"I didn't know how many marshmallows you'd want so I gave you a bowl to pick from," she said, taking her spot on the other side of Mia.

The girl stared at her brother. "Why didn't you tell me Mommy and Daddy are dead?"

"Because you talk too much." Jayden glanced at Ryan.

Shandra didn't understand but saw the corner of Ryan's mouth twitch. Evidently, it had been a subject they'd talked about in the bedroom.

"I don't talk too much!" Mia shoved the hair off her forehead with her small hand and glared at her twin.

"Let's have breakfast so Ryan can get to work

finding out what happened to your parents, and we can…" Shandra didn't know if it was a good idea to run to their house and get them clothes.

"Have another no school day," Ryan said. He studied her over the tops of the children's heads. "Maybe you and Lil could take them riding or hiking. Jayden likes to hike."

"That would all be fun," Shandra said. "But they don't fit in any clothes we have other than the t-shirts they are wearing right now." She raised her eyebrows.

"Gotcha. I'll take care of that." Ryan walked out of the kitchen talking on his phone.

"I want to go to school," Mia said.

"I don't," Jayden said, digging into his cinnamon roll.

"We'll have fun and I can get your school work from your teacher. It's going to be best to keep you here for a few days." At least she assumed that was Ryan's idea since he suggested the no school and riding and hiking. She was dying to know what Jayden had told him. She'd learned since meeting Ryan's nieces and nephews that if Jayden told Ryan something in confidence, he wouldn't tell her. While a lot of kids couldn't keep secrets, which, she had a feeling was Mia – Jayden appeared to be a safe that needed a special combination lock to open. And apparently, her husband had figured it out.

"Where do you think Ryan went?" Jayden asked, glancing over his shoulder.

"To make a call that I imagine has something to do with getting your clothes."

Ryan strode back in the room. "Deputy Speaks will go by your house and bring your clothes and toys here."

He sat down and scooped up a bite of eggs.

"Why can't we go get them? He won't find my secret garden where my doll is hidden." Mia scooted sideways on her chair and faced Ryan.

"Tell me where it is and I'll make sure Deputy Speaks finds it," Ryan put his fork down and pulled out his phone.

"I can't tell you."

The pleading in her voice tugged at Shandra's heart. "Why can't you tell Ryan?" she asked.

"Because it's secret." Tears trickled down her cheeks. "Mommy told me to never tell anyone."

Shandra spun her chair and peered at her husband. His gaze rested on the child.

"Mia, your mommy is gone. I bet she would want you to tell Ryan about the secret place," Shandra said.

The child spun her chair to stare at Shandra. "Why would she want me to tell?"

"Dummy…"

"It's not nice to call your sister names," Ryan said in a stern voice.

"Sorry," Jayden apologized.

"Do you know about the secret place?" Ryan asked Jayden.

The boy shook his head. "It was a girl secret. That's what Mommy said when I wanted to know where it was." He stared at his sister. "You can tell. Mommy won't know anyway."

Mia stirred her eggs with her fork.

"Sharing your mom's secret won't make her mad. I'm sure since you don't have her any more she would like you to have your favorite doll." Shandra put a hand on the child's back and rubbed.

"It's the roses behind the house. You can crawl into them from the side by the tree." Mia put her fork down. "I'm not hungry."

Shandra felt for the child. Not only had she lost her parents but now she felt as if she were betraying her mom. "Thank you. I'm sure you will find comfort in having your doll."

Mia slid off the chair and wandered out of the kitchen. Sheba followed behind her.

Jayden dropped marshmallows in his hot chocolate. "Daddy said Mia and Mommy were two peas. They liked secrets and driving him crazy."

Shandra's lips twitched at the comment. But she also wondered what their mother had been secretive about and why it would drive her husband crazy.

~*~

Sheriff Oldham, Huckleberry Police Chief Sandberg, and a Weippe County Children's Services contact sat in the backroom of the Huckleberry Police Station. Ryan had been surprised when Sheriff Oldham called and told him to be at the HP Station at nine. Now he was even more surprised that his superior had organized this meeting.

"When Ryan called me last night and said he had the Woodcock children and would take them to his home, I knew they were in good hands. That's why I waited until this morning to contact Children's Services," Oldham said.

"I don't care if they were in good hands. Detective Greer should have called us. It's protocol," Mrs. Wagner, the social worker said.

"The children were scared, tired, and hungry. We were strangers to them but Shandra's big fluffy dog was the perfect thing to calm them both down." Ryan wanted to pacify the social worker in hopes she would let them keep the children longer.

Oldham laughed. "Who knew that big coward was good for something."

Ryan grinned at the sheriff. He'd seen how cowardly Sheba could be. "Yeah. She was who helped the children open up a bit." Ryan sobered and said, "The boy saw both bodies. He knows information that could put him in danger." He turned to the sheriff. "I was going to put it all in the report this morning."

"He knows the killers of both his parents?" Sandberg asked.

"He didn't name anyone. Only that he saw the bodies, who picked them up and took them home from the cabin, and who 'supposedly' his mother called before she died." Ryan wasn't giving out any names or saying more with Mrs. Wagner present.

"All the more reason for us to put him in Foster Care," the woman said.

"You can put him in the system as long as you leave out where he's staying," Ryan said. "We don't need someone thinking the boy knows more and trying to kill him." He glared at the woman.

"We can't leave the two with anyone who hasn't filled out the proper forms or had a background check." Mrs. Wagner straightened her back to her full five and a half feet and stared up at him.

"I'll call Shandra and have her fill out the forms. I've had a background check run on me and I'm sure it wouldn't take that long to do one on my wife." Ryan realized the minute he stopped talking that he'd just railroaded Shandra into becoming a foster parent for the twins.

Sheriff Oldham opened his mouth, then clamped it shut and turned to the woman. "I think the children staying with Detective Greer and his wife is a good idea. They'll have protection from someone who knows what is going on."

Chief Sandberg led Ryan into his office and sat him down. "You sure you know what you just did?"

"Yeah, I forced my wife to become a foster parent." Ryan ran a hand over his face. "I know she's already connected with the two, but not letting her come to the decision on her own…"

Sandberg slapped his back. "I've had enough run-ins with Shandra to know she's going to do whatever will help the children and your case."

He smiled. "That's true. I better call her and have her come fill out the paperwork."

"What about the kids? Do you think it's a good idea for them to be seen around town?" The chief sat down behind his desk.

"They can stay at the ranch with Lil. She has a soft spot for animals and kids. No one would want to cross her to get to the twins." Ryan had a feeling this arrangement would be good for all of them, with Lil having just lost her last tie to her family and past.

"Call Shandra and I'll make sure Mrs. Wagner stays in town so they can meet and Shandra can fill out the forms for a background check." Sandberg rose from his chair and disappeared out the door.

Ryan tapped Shandra's name on his phone and listened to it ring.

"Hey, I didn't expect to hear from you so soon," Shandra answered, sounding out of breath.

"What are you doing?" Ryan smiled at the happiness in his wife's voice.

"We were giving the kids a ride on Apple and Duke. Did you learn anything more?"

"Not yet. I haven't had time. The sheriff called me to the Huckleberry Police Station." He went on to tell her about Mrs. Wagner.

"She can't take them somewhere else! They're comfortable here. And Sheba helps them."

"I'd hoped you'd say that. I told them we'd fill out foster parent paperwork. You'll need a background check. Are you okay with that?" He held back his enthusiasm to not sway her if she wasn't comfortable.

"That's a wonderful idea! I can be in town in an hour. Oh wait. My Jeep is in town."

"Have Lil and the kids bring you to town, but she'll need to take them back to the ranch. It's not a good idea for them to be seen too much." Ryan didn't need to say more than that. Shandra had helped him with enough homicide investigations to know witnesses were best kept away from potential suspects.

"But what about the aunt? Won't she want the children?" Shandra asked.

"She may, but until this investigation is finished, she is a suspect and won't be able to see the kids." Ryan would make sure Mrs. Wagner knew that as well.

"And the grandparents? The ones they don't care for?" Shandra asked.

"They are on my list to call this morning. I'll feel them out."

"I'll tell everyone we need to go to town. I'll be there soon."

The connection went dead and Ryan smiled. He

should have known his wife wouldn't mind him offering her up as a foster parent. Especially, when the children had been shown to her by her grandmother in a dream.

Chapter Ten

Shandra sat across from Mrs. Wagner in a backroom of the Huckleberry Police Station. The small woman had variegated gray hair and a steely manner.

"I'm not anxious to allow you to keep the children when I feel as if I've been strong-armed by the sheriff, the chief of police, and your husband," Mrs. Wagner said.

"I only want what is best for the children. Jayden and Mia are dealing with their loss. My dog has been a help to them both. She loves hugs and is a good listener. We also have horses which were my sounding board during my youth. I can't think of a better place than Huckleberry Mountain for two young children to start over." Shandra smiled at the woman's pinched face.

"Fill out this paperwork, please." Mrs. Wagner handed her a half inch thick stack of papers. "You'll also need your husband's information and his signature."

"Can I fill out his information and then get his signature from him?" Shandra stared at the paperwork.

"Yes. That will work. I have a visit to make. I shouldn't be more than an hour." Mrs. Wagner stood. "If I don't have the paperwork when I leave Huckleberry, the children will go with me."

Shandra nodded and pulled out her wallet. She wouldn't be able to fill out all of Ryan's information if they required driver's license numbers.

Once the woman left the room, Shandra gave her ten minutes to make sure she was out of the building before going in search of her husband. He had to know his information was needed to fill out these forms.

He sat in a small office talking on a phone.

"Yes, I understand, you've been gone for several months. I thought since you lived close to your son half of the year, you might know who would have a grudge against him." He listened and motioned for Shandra to enter the room.

"Mr. Woodcock, I told you your son and his wife are dead and you haven't once asked about the children."

Shandra scowled. Why wouldn't a grandparent be concerned for the children's safety?

"I see. And when did you have this discussion with Andie? When the twins were born. Okay. Thank you." He paused, listening. "We'll let you know when the bodies will be released." He hung up the phone, rubbing a hand over his face.

"That call was tough."

"Frustrating is more like it. They don't care about

their grandkids. When the children were born, they told Andie, Jessica's sister, that if something happened to the parents, they wouldn't stand in her way to take care of Jayden and Mia."

"They don't understand that a caring family face would be good for the two right now?" Shandra had a hard time tamping down the anger she felt.

"Apparently not." He stood. "I need to go talk to the sister and Mrs. Webb."

"Wait. You need to fill out the information I don't know on this form. Mrs. Wagner said I had to have it all filled out when she comes back in an hour or she'll take the twins."

Ryan plopped down in the chair and held out his hand.

Shandra handed him the pages that had information she didn't know. "Just fill out the things I don't know. Driver's license and some background things from when you were in Chicago."

He glanced down the two pages and filled in lines. "That should be it. If you come across something else either text or call." Ryan stood, kissed her on the head. "We're doing the right thing stepping in for those two."

She smiled up at her husband. "Yes, we are. Go find out who killed their parents."

Ryan stared down at her. "You aren't going to make up an excuse to come with me?"

"I have paperwork to finish." She bent her head and started filling out the form.

~*~

Ryan decided to talk to Mrs. Webb first, since she lived in Huckleberry. He was still hoping that the twins were going to keep Shandra from digging into the murders. She'd shown no curiosity about who he was visiting, she'd been so intent on getting the paperwork done to keep the kids. If having children would keep her out of harm, this foster thing might be good.

He walked up to the one-story house with an immaculate yard. It sat half a mile down the road beyond Webb Automotive Repair shop at the west edge of Huckleberry.

Knocking on the door started a small dog yapping.

The door opened, revealing a woman in her forties with a trim body, bleached blonde hair, and wary eyes. She held the still yapping shaggy-haired dog in one arm.

"Hello?"

Ryan held up his badge. "Detective Greer with the Weippe Sheriff's Department."

"Crystal, shhhh." She grasped the dog's muzzle with her free hand and whispered in its ear. When she released her hand, the dog just stared at him.

"Why are you here?" She didn't offer to invite him into the house.

"I'm investigating the death of Mitch Woodcock."

"You should go to the shop and talk to my husband. Mitch worked for him." She started to back up and close the door.

"But you were the one at the cabin the day he died."

She dropped the dog to the floor and walked into the house.

Ryan followed, closing the front door behind him.

The woman stood in the middle of a living room that looked right out of one of the magazines Shandra brought home for ideas for her vases. Everything was in its place and not a speck of dust anywhere. A 180 of the conditions the Woodcocks had lived in.

"How did you know I was at the cabin?" She sat down on a chair his mom called a Queen Anne. Her back was straight. Her gaze zeroed in on him. Only the slight shaking of her left hand on the arm of the chair showed she was nervous.

"The kids were with Mitch on the east side of Huckleberry Mountain. We found them two miles behind their home, ten miles from Warner. They couldn't walk that far. I asked them who drove them home." He held up a hand before she could deny it. "We also found the footprints and car tracks of where you met them, led them to your car, and drove them home."

"Well." She clutched her hands on her lap, staring down at them. "I had an appointment with Mitch at the cabin. When I arrived, I found him…" She leaned over, plucked a tissue from a box on the table next to the chair, and dabbed at her eyes. "He was dead when I arrived."

"What time was that?" Ryan pulled out his notepad.

"One."

"On Sunday?"

She shook her head. "Saturday."

That didn't fit with the time frame Jayden told him. "It was Saturday?"

Mrs. Webb stared at him. "I know my days of the week, detective. It was Saturday."

"Why were you meeting Mitch at the cabin?" Ryan didn't like the idea of asking Jayden if he'd been correct about the day, but it was going to be necessary.

"He'd called me. Wanted to see if I knew why my husband fired him." She'd dropped her gaze back to her hands in her lap.

"Why would he talk to you and not Mr. Webb?"

"Richard can be hard to talk to. Especially if he has it in his mind he's right." She peered into his eyes. "Richard could be a total dick when he thought someone had screwed him over."

"What did he think Mitch had done?" Ryan watched her closely.

"Who knows. I'm sure whatever it was Mitch didn't do it. He didn't want to lose his job. That wife of his couldn't keep a job, and they had the two children to raise." When talking about the wife, there was a flicker of distaste in her expression.

"Why did Mitch call you? And why did you go?" Ryan had a feeling the woman and her husband's employee may have been fooling around and that could be why the man was fired.

"He thought maybe I could get Richard to unfire him, I guess. I went because I felt sorry for the kids and Mitch." She shrugged but kept her eyelids lowered.

"How did you know the kids were wandering around in the forest?" Ryan could dig up the dirt on Mitch and the woman.

"Mitch always took them to the cabin on the weekends. It was like he knew the kids needed a break from their mother. And he didn't want to spend two full days with her." There was the distaste. Only this time it was in her tone and her facial expression.

"How did you know he always took the kids to the cabin on the weekends?" Ryan studied her closely. Her cheeks darkened. Her eyelids remained at half-mast as she stalled.

"Did you go up there on the weekends and visit Mitch? Was that why he asked the kids to go for a hike? Because he was having an affair with you?" She didn't deny it, so he pushed on. "Were you meeting him as usual and… he got angry because you couldn't or wouldn't help him? Maybe he said he'd tell your husband about you two if you didn't?"

"No! I could care less what Richard thinks of me. I showed up at the usual time. Everything was quiet. I figured Mitch had sent the kids out, like he always did and he was waiting for me." She scrunched her eyes closed. "He was waiting. But there was blood everywhere and his body was…" She put her hands to her face. "I haven't been able to get that sight out of my mind since Saturday." Her body visibly shuddered.

"Did you walk into the cabin or touch anything?" Ryan figured they were going to find her prints if she'd been a frequent visitor to the cabin, but he wasn't going to tell her that.

"I only opened the door, saw poor Mitch, and backed out. I walked around for nearly an hour before I found the two kids. It took me another twenty minutes to talk them into letting me take them home." She peered at him. "Are they okay? I heard the mother killed herself. Was it because of Mitch's death? She would never have been able to handle those two children on her own. She could barely keep herself together."

"Were the children together when you found them?" Ryan had wanted to believe everything Jayden told him but if he said his father was dead on Sunday and this woman said Saturday, he wondered if the boy had seen his father's body before or after the woman did.

Mrs. Webb pulled another tissue from the box, blew her nose, and nodded. "They, no, the boy came walking up from a different direction as I came upon the girl."

Jayden said he heard the shot and went to the cabin and saw his dad. That meant either the woman shot Mitch or she arrived right after the man was shot.

"What time did you arrive at the cabin?"

"I told you… one."

"And that was the usual time you arrived at the cabin?" The time line, besides the boy saying it happened Sunday, wasn't lining up.

"Yes. I would arrive around one, after he'd fed the kids lunch and sent them out to play."

"They didn't know you came around to the cabin on Saturdays? Couldn't have told their mom about the woman who showed up?" He found it hard to believe this affair hadn't gone unnoticed by the two children they'd found in the woods last night.

"He told them he took naps after lunch. If they happened to come back before I left, he'd dress and walk into the other room and take them for a hike and I'd leave."

"And he never said the kids knew anything?" Ryan studied her.

"No. He said neither the kids or Jessica suspected a thing." She sat up straight. "If Richard had found out, Mitch would have been fired a long time ago. We only saw each other at the cabin and only on Saturdays when Richard was hunting or golfing."

"Did you ever go to the shop during working

hours?" Ryan found it hard to believe in a community this small that they'd kept the affair a secret.

"Yes. And Mitch called me Mrs. Webb and didn't linger anywhere near me. His job was the security he had for those kids. He loved them." She dabbed at her eyes. "It was his loyalty to them that first caught my eye. I figured a man who cared that much for his children would be a man who wouldn't talk about an affair and would have a gentle touch." She sniffed and stood. "I have to make Richard's lunch and take it over to him."

"If you want to make it, I can take it over. That's my next stop."

Her mouth opened and she shook her head. "No. I don't want him knowing you talked to me. He doesn't know about Mitch and I, and I don't want him to know. I have a reputation to uphold, one that would be ruined with a divorce."

Ryan let himself out of the house thinking what a poor woman to remain in a loveless marriage for the sake of her reputation. She'd probably be shocked to learn other people knew what she'd been doing. Someone must have known. He couldn't think of any other reason for Mitch to be dead.

His phone buzzed as he slid behind the wheel of his SUV. "Greer."

"This is Speaks. You might want to come over to the Woodcock residence. When I crawled in the rosebush for the girl's doll, I found something else."

Chapter Eleven

Mrs. Wagner returned to the police station later than an hour. Shandra was thankful for the delay. She'd had to text Ryan for answers and he'd not responded right away. She sat in the lobby of the Huckleberry Police Station thankful that this time she wasn't a suspect in a murder. A smile settled on her lips, remembering how she'd met Ryan during a murder investigation and he'd ruled her out before the Huckleberry Police had.

"You have a satisfied expression," Hazel, the retired woman who worked the dispatch during the day, said.

"Hopefully, I filled out this stack of papers to Mrs. Wagner's satisfaction." Shandra stood and walked over to the dispatch desk. "Do you know anything about Mitch and Jessica Woodcock? You know good things I can bring up to help the twins remember their parents?"

Hazel smiled. "That's nice of you. You could talk to Mitch's parents, though they have never been hands-on parents. When they should have pushed Mitch to use his football scholarship to go to college, they just sat back and let him 'figure it out himself.' That was their thing. They are kind of late blooming hippies, if you ask me." She waved a hand and stood. "Want a cup of coffee?"

"No, thank you. I'm going over to Ruthie's for lunch as soon as I can pass these papers off to Mrs. Wagner." Shandra moved to sit back down in the chair to wait when the door opened.

Mrs. Wagner's eyes widened at the sight of her holding the sheath of paperwork. "Did you finish?"

"Yes. Everything is filled out, and Hazel pulled up Ryan's background check and said mine should be ready by tomorrow." Shandra placed Ryan's background check on the top of the stack of papers.

"Thank you. You are very thorough." The social worker took the papers and shoved them in her tote bag.

"I am. And so is Ryan. The Woodcock twins will be in good hands. Their safety means everything to us." Shandra waved her fingers at Hazel and strode out of the police station. She didn't know why, but Mrs. Wagner pushed her buttons.

Shandra walked the two and a half blocks to Ruthie's where her Jeep was still parked out front.

"Shandra, I wondered if you'd stop in when you picked up your Jeep." Ruthie was serving a couple at a booth by the door. Little Donnie grinned and squealed from his mom's back.

"I was hoping my husband would join me, but he texted as I walked in that he won't be able to make it."

She sat in her favorite booth toward the back of the diner, in a corner where she could watch everyone who entered. She enjoyed people watching when she ate alone. Something she'd done for years until she met Ryan.

After depositing the burger baskets on the table by the door, Ruthie walked over, her order pad ready. "What'll you have?"

"I would like a large caramel milk shake, a big juicy cheeseburger, and a basket of sweet potato fries with your special sauce." She could have just said her usual but she felt like celebrating. Saying everything out loud seemed more like celebrating than uttering two words.

"My, you are in a good mood. Did you finish a project?" Ruthie asked as she hurried to put her order up in line.

"No, something better." Shandra smiled at her friend.

Ruthie called into the back, "Marcy, come take orders." She swung the baby backpack off and hurried back to Shandra's booth. "What? Are you pregnant?" Her friend's smile stretched across her lovely face as she slid onto the seat across from her and placed Donnie on her lap.

"No. Better. I just filled out papers to be a foster parent."

Some of Ruthie's enthusiasm slid off her face. "Foster parent? Are you sure that's what you want to do?"

"Right now, I am completely sure. You heard about Mitch and Jessica Woodcock?"

"Yes. They had two children. Twins."

"Yes. Ryan and I found them wandering around behind their house last night. We brought them home. They are two wonderful kids that deserve to heal with help. They've already made a connection with Sheba—"

Ruthie laughed. "You mean Sheba is convinced you brought them home for her to play with."

"Tomato, too-mot-toe," Shandra took the shake Marcy brought out to the table. "They are all good for one another. And Lil could use the distraction right now. You should have seen her face when we brought the two home last night."

"I can't deny you are excited about this. And Ryan?"

"It was his idea. We can keep them safe—"

"Safe? Why aren't they safe?" Ruthie lowered her voice and leaned across the table.

"Jayden may have seen or knows more than he's told Ryan so far. Which means, whoever killed his father and mother may want to keep him quiet."

"Oh my! Do you want Maxwell to set up one of the cameras at your place that he set up at ours?"

"You mean a trail cam?" Shandra had listened to Maxwell extoll all the wonderful things he'd been seeing on the three trail cameras he'd set up on the edges of the Treat property several miles down the county road from Ryan and Shandra's.

"You never know. You might pick up if someone is looking around trying to find a way to get to the boy." Ruthie leaned back as Marcy delivered the burger and fries. Her friend stole a couple fries and slid out of the booth. "I better get back to work. Let me know if you want Maxwell to install one."

Shandra waved a fry before popping it into her mouth. An animal camera might be a good idea now that they would have children around. She'd see what Ryan thought.

~*~

The ground under the rose bush was musty with decaying leaves. Ryan was glad Speaks hadn't pulled what he'd found out of the hiding spot.

"I even left the doll," Speaks said from behind him.

"Nice touch." Ryan clicked the camera, taking photos of the entrance to the rose bush hideout and photos of the doll sleeping on a box with a pocket pack of tissues for a pillow and a washrag for a blanket.

"What prompted you to look in the box?" Ryan asked.

The deputy cleared his throat. "Thought it might have been a box of clothes for the doll. Didn't find much for clothes for the kids or toys in the house."

Shandra had already mentioned taking the twins to Missoula to buy clothes and toys. He tried to remind her they may not have the children very long if the family stepped forward. "Then Jayden and Mia will have what they need when they go to their family." She'd mentioned Missoula, knowing he wouldn't want them seen around Weippe County. It would be too easy for the killer to find a chance to hurt them.

After taking photos of the doll on the box, Ryan handed the doll, pillow, and washrag out to Speaks. He unlatched the metal box and whistled. "This looks like five grand worth of meth."

"That's what I thought," Speaks said.

Ryan took more photos, closed the lid and dragged the box out of the bush. "Have you heard anything about the victim being a drug dealer?" he asked, standing with the box tucked under his arm.

"I haven't heard a thing other than she was a user. Never a dealer." Speaks led the way back to the vehicles. "Want to put the clothes and toys in your rig?"

"Yeah, save you a trip to Huckleberry." At the vehicles, Ryan placed the box of meth in Speaks' trunk while the deputy put the doll on top of a cardboard box of clothes, a couple toy cars, and two stuffed animals.

"That's all that was in the kid's room?" Ryan asked, taking the box from him.

"All I saw in the whole house." Speaks tone spoke volumes to his sadness over the few items. "Those two will be lucky to have you and Shandra."

"Don't go thinking they're staying with us forever. We only signed foster papers. Anyone of their family members could step forward and want them after we solve the homicides." Ryan had reminded Shandra of that fact when she became excited about signing the papers.

"Well, then they are lucky to have you two for whatever time they have." Speaks closed the trunk. "I'll get this to the forensic lab. Maybe they can learn something about its origin."

"Good idea. I still have to interview the sister. She's in Warner. I'll be following behind you for a bit." Ryan put the box in the back of his SUV and slid in behind the wheel.

A text dinged.

Signed all the paperwork, handed it over to Mrs. Wagner, and had lunch at Ruthie's. Headed home now.

K. I have the toys and clothing. I may be late for dinner. Will let you know.

See you then!

He smiled, wondering how Lil got along with the two kids during Shandra's absence.

Chapter Twelve

Driving up the sweeping driveway of the Teague residence, Ryan wondered why the woman hadn't been on their doorstep demanding her niece and nephew be handed over to her. She'd seemed distressed thinking the father might have run off with them, then according to dispatch, she never once called in to see if the children had been found. This morning, when he'd requested Cathleen call from the Sheriff's Office and let Mrs. Teague know the children had been found, she'd reported that the woman thanked her for calling and didn't ask about the children's welfare.

The Teague house had plenty of room for two children. From what he'd read about the Teagues, they didn't have any. Mr. Teague worked for a commercial insurance agency in Coeur d'Alene.

The door opened before he reached the porch. A slender man in his forties stood on the threshold, blinking at him through nerdy glasses.

"Hello, may I help you?"

Ryan showed his badge and introduced himself. He held out a hand. "Are you Mr. Teague?"

The man shook. "Yes, Bradley Teague. What did you need to speak to my wife about? She hasn't been in good health."

"Can we step inside?" Ryan motioned to the open door.

"Yes, of course." Mr. Teague backed up, making room for Ryan to enter. "What is this about?"

Ryan studied the man. He seemed genuinely confused. "Your sister-in-law and her husband's bodies were found yesterday."

Mr. Teague blinked quickly. "Jessica and Mitch? How? Why?" He ran a hand over his sandy colored hair. "What about the twins? Are they—"

"They're safe. When was the last time you saw either Jessica or Mitch?" Ryan pulled out his notepad. He wondered at the wife not telling her husband about the deaths.

"Let me think. I don't have as much interaction with them as Andie. I'm in Coeur d'Alene half of the week." He took his glasses off and cleaned them with a pristine white handkerchief he'd pulled from a pocket. "I believe I saw Jessica and the kids a week ago. They were here visiting when I came home. Mitch… We ran in difference circles. He worked at the auto shop and spent weekends drinking beer and hunting with his friends." The man made hunting and drinking beer sound like felonies.

"A week ago, when you last saw Jessica, how was she acting?" Ryan studied the man. He was too thoughtful before he commented. It made Ryan wonder if Teague chose his words wisely as he made something up.

"Acting? Like Jessica. I believe she begged money off of Andie and then drove off." The man didn't hide one bit of the animosity he felt toward his sister-in-law.

"Did she come here often asking for money?"

"At least once a month. If she'd kicked her drug habit, cleaned up, and got a job, she wouldn't have had to beg her sister for money." Mr. Teague waved to a fancy couch. "Please, have a seat. I'll go find Andie."

Ryan sat. The second the man disappeared through a door, he was up prowling the room, looking at photographs. There were many of the husband and wife on various vacations from the background scenery. There was one with the two sisters when they were high school age. Andie was the prettier of the two and knew it. She overshadowed her sister in the photo. There was one Christmas photo of the Woodcock family. The twins looked to be about three years old. They appeared a happy family. The adults staring into one another's eyes adoringly, and the children smiling at the camera.

He heard hushed voices and hurried back to his seat on the couch.

The couple entered. Mr. Teague sat in a straight-backed chair, and Mrs. Teague sat on the opposite end of the couch.

Ryan held out his hand. "Mrs. Teague, I spoke with you yesterday. I'm sorry for your loss, but I have some questions to ask you."

"Do you have any idea what happened to Jessica and Mitch?" the woman asked.

"Not yet."

"And Jayden and Mia, are they okay? I called to see about taking them and I was told they were with a foster family until the murders are cleared up. I don't understand why I can't take them."

Ryan could tell she was fishing. He wasn't going to bite, knowing she hadn't asked about them according to dispatch. "I'm sure the authorities know what is best at this time. I'm curious why you didn't tell your husband about the deaths? I called and told you about them yesterday."

Her gaze flicked to her husband, who scowled, studying her. "He returned late last night. I'd already gone to bed. And this morning, he was on the phone. I never had time."

Watching the husband, it was plain that he didn't agree with her comment, but he didn't voice his thoughts.

"When was the last time you saw either your sister or your brother-in-law?" Ryan poised his pen over his notepad and studied the woman, with the husband in his peripheral vision.

"Mitch, it's been weeks. He works at the repair place and then weekends he takes the kids and goes hiking. At least that's what Jessica says…said." She pulled out a woman's handkerchief and dabbed at her eyes.

"You don't believe he took the kids hiking every weekend?" Ryan asked.

"Did I say every weekend? I don't know what I'm saying half the time anymore." She peered at her husband with teary eyes.

"My wife has gone through some trauma lately and she really shouldn't be upset," Mr. Teague stood as if trying to get Ryan to also stand.

"I'm sorry. But I have two homicides to solve. When was the last time you saw your sister?"

Mr. Teague slowly folded back down onto the chair.

"A week ago. She came here asking for money. She said the kids needed it for a field trip but I could tell she needed a fix." The woman didn't show any sympathy toward her sister.

"Who was the oldest?"

"She was. Why?" Mrs. Teague scowled at him.

"Didn't she take care of you when your mother died and your father went to prison?" Ryan had read all about the family's history. From where he sat, Andie Teague had come out of a dysfunctional family on the good side of things.

"Prison? You told me both your parents were dead." Mr. Teague stood up, towering over his wife.

"That's something you two will have to hash out later," Ryan stood. "Why don't you go get your wife a cup of coffee or whatever she drinks."

Mr. Teague glared at him but left the room.

"Mrs. Teague. I know you and Jessica didn't grow up in a normal family setting. I know that she didn't finish school so you could. All I'm asking is your cooperation in trying to find out who killed her."

The woman's hand shook as she pushed strands off her face. "You ruined my life by coming in here and telling my husband the family I came from. Why should I help you?"

"You're not helping me. You're getting justice for your sister. The one who ruined her life, trying to make yours better." He stared into her eyes. She knew that was the truth. And he had a feeling that was why she gave her older sister money when she asked. "You say you saw her a week ago. Jayden said she called you on Sunday. Did you go to the house to see her?" He hoped that saying Sunday didn't confuse the woman. But that was what Jayden said. He had to determine if the seven-year-old was wrong or Mrs. Webb was deliberately trying to mix things up.

"No. She didn't call me on Sunday." She shook her head. "Why was she going to call me?"

"I don't know." In honesty, he didn't. He only had a child's word for what might or might not have happened.

"Was your sister also dealing drugs along with using them?"

A crash at the doorway to the room, swung their attention to Mr. Teague. He stood with his hands at his sides, his mouth open, and his eyes riveted to his wife. The cups, coffee, and milk spilled across a tray at his feet. He stepped over the tray and strode up to Mrs. Teague. He reached down, grabbed her by her upper arms and hauled her to her feet. "Your sister was dealing drugs? And I find out your father is in prison. What else haven't you told me?"

"Nothing! That's all the dirty secrets I have. Well, except Jessica dealing. I didn't know about that." Her head swiveled and she peered at Ryan. "Why would she get money from me if she was dealing drugs?"

"Good question." Ryan stood. "I'll contact you if I have any other questions." He walked out of the house. While he was a pretty good judge of character, he didn't see Mr. Teague hitting his wife. He could see the man sitting her down and questioning her like a prosecutor but nothing physically violent. The appearances the Teagues kept up might be shattered soon. Having her sister and brother-in-law victims of homicides wouldn't be good for the status they were both desperately trying to keep.

~*~

Sheba bounded out of the barn followed by the two children as Shandra drove out of the trees lining the driveway and up to the barn.

Lil corralled the dog and children while Shandra pulled the vehicle into the barn.

Climbing out of the Jeep, Shandra was bombarded with questions and a big slobbery dog.

"Whoa. Down Sheba. What did you say?" she asked, peering down at Mia who was still jabbering.

"Lil says Lewis is a boy cat and can't have babies, but she might get me a kitten the next time she goes to town. Claude at the feed store has kittens," Mia chattered.

"My, well, as much as I like kittens, if you get one, it will have to be an outside pet, like the horses. One big shaggy dog in the house is enough." Shandra handed a bag of groceries to Jayden and one to Mia. "Help me carry this into the house. I picked up ingredients for spaghetti and ice cream."

"Yay!" both kids yelled and double-stepped toward the back door of the house.

Shandra walked slower with Lil at her side. "Were they any trouble?"

"No. The boy is kind of mopey, but the girl never quits talking." She frowned.

"Why are you frowning?"

"They loved their parents, warts and all, like kids

do, but they have gone without a lot." Lil peeled off at the studio.

Shandra had thought as much when Ryan wouldn't let her see the house or get their things. She found the two children and the dog, pulling items out of the grocery bag.

"Sheba, bed," she scolded the adult dog who had resorted to puppy behavior since the arrival of the twins.

"She was just helping get the groceries out of the bag," Jayden said, his slackened face turning sulky.

"She isn't a person. Her slobbery mouth doesn't need to touch food we're going to eat." Shandra took the items it was obvious Sheba had helped with to the sink and washed off the drool.

The boy started to wander out of the kitchen.

"Jayden, do you know what an ice cream maker looks like?" she asked.

He stopped and stared at her. "I never been to an ice cream factory."

"In the days of the pioneers, before factories and stores were everywhere, people made their own ice cream." Shandra set the washed items in the drainer, picked up the sacks the kids had placed on the floor, and put them on the counter. She pointed to the pantry door. "In the back of the pantry, I think about knee high on a shelf is a wood bucket with a handle that cranks. Would you go in there and get it for me?"

"Are we going to make ice cream?" Mia asked, amazement in her voice.

"We are. But it takes teamwork and strong arms." Shandra finished putting everything away but the ingredients for the ice cream.

Jayden appeared in the pantry doorway, carrying the crank ice cream maker her Aunt Jo gave them as a wedding gift. She'd said it was the same one Ella, Grandmother, had used all of her life to make the cold, sweet treat.

"How does this make ice cream?" he asked, setting the wooden bucket on the counter.

"I was just telling your sister it requires teamwork and strong arms." Shandra pulled out the center piece, took it to the sink, and washed it.

"Why are you cleaning that? It was sitting in that clean room." Jayden twirled the handle on the side of the bucket.

"It might have been sitting inside, but it never hurts to make sure. An insect or something smaller could have crawled in and out of it."

"Yuck! I don't want insect ice cream," Mia said. Her tone must have sounded frightened. Sheba came bounding into the room as if she expected an intruder.

Shandra laughed. Who knew all it took were two children for the cowardly dog to become brave?

"Let's measure our ingredients." They each took turns with the cream, whole milk, sugar, salt, and vanilla. Shandra stirred the mixture and poured it into the center vessel. When it was attached, she walked to the refrigerator and pulled out the bin of ice cubes on the freezer side.

"What's that for?" Mia asked.

"To freeze the ice cream." Shandra poured the ice around the edge between the center vessel and the wooden bucket. She pointed to the handle. "Start turning."

Jayden grabbed the handle first and started

cranking. "This is harder than before. Why did you put the ice in there?"

"The paddle, in the center container with the ice cream, stirs the ingredients to make them smooth and touch the cold sides as the canister spins against the ice, freezing the ingredients. It's better than any ice cream you've ever had. But it takes time. When you get tired, Mia will take over." Shandra put the salt, vanilla, and sugar away and grabbed the box of rock salt in the pantry. She sprinkled it over the ice.

"What does that do?" Mia asked, wistfully studying her brother twirling the handle.

"The salt makes the ice melts. When ice melts it gets colder, freezing the ingredients even more." Shandra placed the box on the counter.

"My arm can't move," Jayden said, backing away from the counter, his right arm hanging at his side.

Mia grabbed the handle and turned it with both hands. "Do we get to eat this when it's done?"

"We'll have it for dessert tonight. I'm sure Ryan would enjoy a bowl."

Jayden sat on the chair. "Do you think he found out who killed Mommy and Daddy today?"

"I'm sure we won't know today. When someone does something as bad as hurting others, they tend to hide behind lies. It takes time to sort out what is the truth and what isn't." She put a hand on the boy's shoulder. "But Ryan always finds the truth." She felt the boy stiffen. Interesting. What had he lied about?

Chapter Thirteen

Webb Automotive Repair appeared closed. Ryan glanced at his watch. 4:30. He read the sign next to the door. Open: 8 am – 5 pm Mon.- Fri. He'd hoped to talk to Webb and the other employees. Finding the drugs in a place that it appeared only Mia and her mother knew about, had him wondering if the husband hadn't known about the drugs or if he had been the one dealing.

He banged on the door and listened. Nothing. The Webbs didn't appear to have a blissful marriage. He doubted the man went home. There were three local bars and three that catered to tourists in Huckleberry. His money was on the ones that didn't cater to tourists.

Two of the local bars were down Second street only a few blocks from the automotive shop.

Ryan drove to the first one. He had Webb's driver's license photo on his phone. Inside the dark bar he scanned the dozen or so people present but didn't see

Webb.

The bartender walked down to the end of the bar near where Ryan stood. "Can I help you?"

"Does Richard Webb come in here to drink?" Ryan stepped up to the bar.

"Not anymore. Tossed him out on his ass when he started causing trouble. Told him to drink and fight elsewhere." The man showed off a prized pair of biceps when he said tossed.

"He drink too much often?" Ryan was slowly piecing together a profile of the automotive shop owner.

"Only when he struck out with a barmaid." The man snickered. "You'd think in a town this size, he'd realize they all know he's married. And why he'd want to bed a woman working at a bar when he's got that hot wife of his at home." Shaking his head, he pointed to the door. "Try Maxi's. I heard he's been trying to hit on the tourist ladies lately."

"Thanks." Ryan had a thought. "Any of the people who work for him in here?"

He nodded to a middle-aged man sipping a beer and watching the one television set in the place. "Ray works for him. Guess he canned Mitch. That's too bad, he needed the money to support those kids."

Ryan studied the bartender. It appeared he didn't know Mitch was dead. "Mitch come in here often?"

"Every Thursday night like clockwork. It's trivia night. He usually won. The prize was twenty-five dollars."

"Was he here this past Thursday?"

"Yeah, like I said, just like clockwork."

"He won't be here this week or any week after that.

He was killed over the weekend." Ryan studied the man the best he could in the dimly lit establishment.

"No, shit! What about Jessica and the kids?" The man seemed to genuinely care about the family. He showed more interest than the victim's sister and brother-in-law.

"Jessica is dead as well."

The bartender slammed a fist down on the counter. Everyone in the place looked their direction.

"You are the first person I've come across in my investigation that seems to care about the family." Ryan slid onto the nearest bar stool. "I could use some help understanding them."

"Steve Ervin, by the way." The bartender put his hand out over the bar.

"Detective Greer, Weippe County Sherriff's Department." Ryan shook hands.

"I figured you were police the questions you asked. Hold on." He walked to the three men sitting at the end of the bar, said something, then called, "Angel! Over here."

A woman in her late twenties with curls piled on her head and dressed in skin tight jeans and t-shirt with a short bookie apron strode to the bar. "What's up, Steve?"

"This is a detective. He just told me that Mitch and Jessica are dead." Steve's voice cracked.

"Why do you think I wanted the night off. I heard it on the radio yesterday." She faced Ryan, her face disfigured by the rage sparking in her eyes. "I didn't care about that low-life whore he married. But Mitch was a good man."

Ryan shook his head. "No one deserves to be

murdered.”

The woman sucked in air then laughed. “Some people do. She was like an anchor around Mitch's neck.”

“Sis, that's no way to talk about Jessica.” Steve glared at his sister.

Ryan had the feeling they each had a thing for the married couple.

“She was nothing and she made him feel like he was nothing.” Angel glared at Ryan as if he caused all of Mitch Woodcock's troubles. “He went to college on a football scholarship. She plays her poor me act, and he drops out of football and out of school. The next thing you know she's pregnant, they're getting married, and the rest of us decent women are left wondering what she had over him to keep him in Huckleberry when all he talked about was getting out of here.”

“She did all she could to give Andie a normal life. You know she quit school so Andie could stay in after their mom died.” Steve crossed his arms and stared at his sister.

“When did Jessica start taking drugs?” Ryan asked.

“When hasn't she?” Angel stared at her brother as if daring him to say anything different.

“Can I get a refill?” a patron shouted.

Angel threw her arms in the air, grimaced, and spun around. Her boot heels clapped on the wood flooring as she stomped her way over to the table.

“My sister was dating Mitch when he dumped her for Andie, Jessica's sister. They went off to college and he came back married to Jessica with the twins. That makes her just a bit sensitive when it comes to Mitch and Jessica.” Steve uncrossed his arms, filled a glass with tap beer and exchanged it for the empty glass when Angel returned. She spun around so fast Ryan was surprised beer didn't slosh out of the glass.

Ryan nibbled on some peanuts and realized it was dinner time and he hadn't let Shandra know he would be late. He pulled out his phone and sent a text. *Running late. Don't wait for me.*

Angel didn't return to the bar. It seemed she didn't have anything more to say about the murdered couple. "Jessica. You seem to be on her side. How well did you know her?" Ryan asked.

"We dated before her mom became sick. Then she dropped everything, went to work, and tried to keep life normal for Andie. Her mom dies, Andie graduates and heads off to college, and the next thing I hear Jessica is Mrs. Mitch Woodcock and they have twins."

"Was she using drugs then?" Ryan wondered if the woman had become a dealer to get her fix and make money to leave a life it seemed she wasn't happy with.

"She didn't start using until after they moved back to Weippe County. She'd come in here on Saturday nights, when Mitch had the kids. She talked about getting out of here and letting Mitch care for his brats." He shook his head. "I guess raising her sister made her not want to be a mother."

Ryan latched onto the 'his brats' comment. He'd have someone dig into Jessica's medical records and see if she actually gave birth to the twins.

~*~

Dinner warmed as they waited for Ryan to come home. Shandra finally sent the kids out to see if Lil needed help feeding the horses. Something was keeping Ryan. He always let her know when he'd be late.

As if reading her mind, the phone dinged. *Running late. Don't wait for me.*

She hoped he had dug up some good information. Shandra walked to the back door, and out to the barn and corral to get the kids for dinner.

Jayden and Mia stood on the second rail from the bottom on the corral watching the horses eat hay.

"Does watching the horses make you hungry?" she asked, walking up behind them.

They both flinched and ducked before slowly turning their heads. Their eyes held a blank stare she could only think of calling distancing. They both seemed to be pulling back their feelings to keep from showing…fear?

"Ryan said he's going to be late and to start eating without him." She waved her hand toward the house. "Come on. There's a lot of spaghetti and ice cream to eat."

Mia was the first to smile and jump down from the fence. "Can Lil eat with us?"

"If she wants to." Shandra was happy that the kids had seen past Lil's gruffness.

"I'll go ask her." Mia ran off, leaving Shandra and Jayden alone.

"Come on," she said, motioning for him to climb down off the fence.

The blankness in his eyes had disappeared. In its place was sorrow. A sorrow so deep, she felt it like a heavy weight in her stomach.

"Is there something you want to tell me?" Shandra asked, moving to stand alongside him, placing her arms on the top rail of the corral, and staring at the horses.

"I told Ryan it was Sunday when we were with

Daddy at the cabin and he was shot. It was Saturday. I didn't want Mommy to get in trouble cuz she wasn't home when Mrs. Webb dropped us off after she found us. When she did come home and we were there, she was mad. She didn't believe me that Daddy was dead. She said he dumped us to run off with his girlfriend." Jayden's voice lowered. "Daddy didn't have as many girlfriends as Mommy had boyfriends."

Shandra put a hand on his thin arm. "Do you want me to tell Ryan for you?"

He nodded his head. "I don't like talking bad about Mommy, but there were times when I didn't like her much."

"You comin' to eat?" Lil called from the corner of the barn.

"Yeah." Shandra tipped his face to peer into his eyes. "We all have moments like that about our parents."

He must have seen the honesty in her face, because he nodded once and hopped off the fence before speeding toward the house.

She knew a lot about a mother's betrayal. Her own mother had married the man who'd killed Shandra's father. Then they'd made her think her father's family wanted nothing to do with her, and her mother had pushed her relationship with a college professor who turned out to be a sadistic womanizer. Oh, she knew all about a mother's betrayal.

Chapter Fourteen

Shandra settled the kids in the master bedroom to watch a movie. It was the only room in the house with a TV. The television had shown up when Ryan moved in. He liked watching movies in bed. Shandra had to agree it was a fun and lazy way to spend a couple of hours now and then.

She'd dug out a box of kid's movies she'd picked up for when Ryan's nieces and nephews came over. She learned while starting the movie, the two had only watched tv when they were at their aunt's or grandparents. The Woodcock family hadn't had a television set.

Shandra was cleaning up the dinner dishes when Sheba started barking and ran through the house to the back door. It wasn't her intruder alert, it was her happy, Ryan's home bark.

"Go get him," Shandra said, opening the back door.

The shaggy mutt bounded out toward the lean-to on the barn where Ryan kept his vehicle.

She went back to cleaning up and setting the food that had been warming for him, out on the island.

The door opened, Sheba ran straight down the hall and into the master bedroom. Giggles echoed through the great room. Great! She would have to change the bedding before they could go to sleep tonight. She had a feeling Sheba had launched herself onto the middle of the bed.

"Thank you for texting," Shandra said, when Ryan walked into the kitchen after depositing his computer on the dining room table in the great room.

"Sorry it was a bit late. I was in the middle of questioning someone when I realized the time." He kissed her on the cheek and sat down to the spaghetti, bread, and salad on his plate. "This smells and looks good." He nodded toward the great room. "I take it the twins are in our room, since that's where Sheba ran to."

She laughed. "Yes. I really think Ruthie has it right. She says Sheba thinks we brought the kids home for her to play with. Like toys."

Ryan laughed. "She has been acting that way." He sobered. "I learned more about their parents today."

"Enough to help figure out who killed them?" Shandra asked, sitting down beside him with a glass of wine and setting a bottle of beer in front of him.

"Not yet. But I'm getting a pretty good picture of them. I also asked for medical records to be pulled."

Shandra inhaled and choked on the sip of wine. She coughed and Ryan patted her on the back. When she could talk, she asked, "Do you think Mitch was abusive?"

"No. If anything he was the calm and loving parent from what I've heard so far." Ryan twisted his fork in the spaghetti on his plate. "There was a comment made that makes me think Jessica may not be their biological mother." He said this in a low whisper.

"Really?" She thought about what Jayden had told her. "Jayden fessed up that he didn't tell you the truth. They were at the cabin Saturday and that's when their dad was killed. He didn't want to say that because when Mrs. Webb dropped them off, Jessica wasn't home. She didn't get home until Sunday and was mad that they were there. She made a comment about their dad dropping them off to go to see his girlfriend. He said she didn't believe him that Mitch was dead."

Ryan nodded. "Now I know that Mrs. Webb was telling me the truth. I wondered who was lying. What made Jayden tell you the truth?"

She smiled at him over the rim of her wine glass. "A comment I made." She kissed his cheek. "I may be good at this parenting stuff."

He kissed her lips. "I never had a doubt."

Mia hurried into the room. "Can we have more ice cream?" She hopped around like she wanted to ask but also wanted to hurry back to the movie.

"I'll go pause the movie and you and Jayden may eat ice cream here in the kitchen." Shandra strode out of the kitchen.

Ryan smiled at the girl. "Did you have fun today?"

She grinned and climbed up onto the chair beside him. "I did. Lil gave us a ride on Oliver and let us brush all the horses."

Every girl he'd ever known, including his sisters, loved horses. "I bet the horses liked that." He continued eating his dinner.

"They did. They nickered when we came in for lunch." She stared at the plate of garlic bread in front of his plate.

"You can have a piece of bread, I'm not going to eat it all," he said, pushing the plate closer to her.

"One piece is all we get and we've had sandwiches for lunch and bread for dinner." She clasped her hands, resting them on the counter, and placing her chin on her hands, staring at the bread.

"We don't have a limit to how many pieces of bread you can have." Ryan pushed the plate closer.

She reached out, like a dog hiding in an alley and grasped the bread.

"What are you doing?" Jayden asked, walking up beside his sister and taking the bread from her.

"I told her she could have that," Ryan said, motioning for the boy to give the food back to his sister. "Here you can have all you want to eat. You just have to ask to make sure it's not too close to mealtime."

Shandra walked by and straight to the freezer. "Did you tell Ryan what kind of ice cream we made?"

Jayden climbed up on a stool but was clearly thinking things through and not interested in the merriment Shandra was trying to conjure up.

Ryan decided to let the boy think. "What kind did you make?"

Mia spun to face him, a wad of bread in her mouth. "Thocolate and pharmel."

"Chew what's in your mouth and swallow, then tell Ryan what kind," Shandra said.

Ryan smiled at his wife over the top of the child's head. He'd always known she'd be a much better mother than the one she had.

"Chocolate and caramel. Chocolate for you, because Shandra said you like chocolate and so do Jayden and me and caramel because that's what she likes. And we like it too, now." Mia grinned.

"Then this isn't your first bowl of ice cream tonight?" Ryan asked, and wished he hadn't when she shoved the bowl away and Jayden didn't grab the bowl Shandra handed to him.

"We don't need another bowl," Jayden said, easing off the stool.

"Sit down." Ryan said, standing and joining Shandra on the other side of the island so he could look at the twins at the same time. "What did I just say?" He glanced back and forth between the two children.

"To sit down?" Jayden said.

"Before that, when you took the bread away from your sister."

"That we could eat anything we wanted as long as we asked," Mia chimed in.

"And did you come in the kitchen and ask for ice cream?"

"Yes!" Mia picked up her spoon, ready to dig into the brown dessert with caramel pieces.

"Then you are both welcome to eat it." Ryan studied the boy.

Jayden's gaze stayed steady on Shandra.

Ryan bumped her with his shoulder.

"I think you should be able to eat whenever you want. Didn't I just dish up the ice cream?" Shandra said.

Once she'd agreed, Jayden plunged his spoon into the ice cream.

Ryan had begun to see a pattern with the Woodcock family. Mitch took the kids on his own as much as he could to save them from Jessica, but what he didn't understand was why Mitch stayed with her. From the way Angel at the bar had talked, there were any number of women who would have gladly put up with Mitch's kids to call him theirs. What hold did Jessica have over Mitch? And what had she, or the two of them, done that got them both killed?

Chapter Fifteen

"When do you think the kids should go back to school?" Shandra asked, as she and Ryan dressed the next morning.

"I'd like to keep them here until I can come up with the reason their parents were killed." Ryan straightened from shoving his feet into his cowboy boots. "I learned a lot about the two before they married last night at the bar. By the time I got to Maxie's to talk to Mr. Webb, he'd left. Maxine said he's in there every weeknight to avoid going home."

"Are you going to talk to him at the shop today or wait and talk to him at Maxie's tonight?" Shandra didn't mind Ryan working long hours. She knew he was dedicated to finding those who broke the law.

"I'm going to try to catch him at the shop. He has an employee I also didn't get the chance to talk to last night. He left the bar without me seeing him. The bartender knew a lot about the Woodcocks. His sister was in love with Mitch." He started for the door and stopped. "She didn't act like she knew he'd been having rendezvouses with his boss's wife. She did, however, hate Jessica."

Shandra watched him walk out of the bedroom and across to his laptop on the dining room table. Last night, after eating ice cream, they'd all ended up on the bed watching the rest of the movie. Her heart had ached with happiness seeing the smile on Mia's face as Ryan carried her to the bed in the guest room. She'd been asleep.

Jayden had wandered down the hall drunkenly behind them. Shandra and Sheba had brought up the rear of the group. She'd tucked the kids in and didn't scold Sheba when she'd jumped on the bed and lay down between the two.

The more she learned about the twins, she realized they had been brought up following two different sets of rules. Ones their mother set and ones their father set. That had to be hard for children to know when to do what when they were with each parent.

In the kitchen she started breakfast. If Ryan didn't want them going to school, she'd run to the school this morning and get their work. It would be a shame for them to get behind because of all of this.

~*~

Ryan sat at the dining room table while Shandra made breakfast, and pulled up his work email. He'd sent off requests for a lot of information last night after he'd put the kids to bed. What caught his attention this morning were two reports from the State Lab Forensic Pathology Unit. They were both from Sheila Rickman, a forensic pathologist he'd worked with for several years.

He opened the report for Mitch.

Male, Caucasian, 27, in excellent health. Buckshot blast to the torso. Died between midnight and 3:00 am four days prior to this report. Estimating victim was shot no more than ten feet away according to the size of the wound. BBs pulled from the body suggests a shotgun was used.

Ryan wondered about the shotgun he'd bagged from over the door of the cabin. Was it a pre-meditated homicide and the person arrived at the cabin planning to use the shotgun and put it back? Or had the gun been leaning up somewhere and the gun was shot out of anger and then replaced above the door, meaning whoever used it had been to the cabin before and knew where it belonged. This was opening up a whole new line of thought. He needed to ask Jayden if the shotgun had been hanging up or leaning somewhere.

He opened Jessica's report.

Female, 29, traces of methamphetamine in nostrils and liver damaged due to drug use. Slits on wrists not deep enough to cause death. Toxicology sent to lab. No sign of struggle. Vomiting had occurred, traces of stomach contents found in trachea and esophagus.

Ryan studied the last part. The victim had vomited. He hadn't noticed that at the scene. Had someone cleaned it up? Jayden or someone else?

He studied his inbox. Nothing from forensics on the shotgun or the meth they found in the box under the roses.

"Breakfast is ready," Shandra called from the kitchen.

The sound of small feet running down the hall made him smile. It was time for them to have children in the house. It was evident Sheba wanted children.

He walked into the kitchen and found the big furry mutt sitting between the stools the kids sat on. Sheba could put her chin on the counter but she was using her manners and waiting for food to fall. Which it did. He'd been around his nieces and nephews enough to know food fell on the floor when kids ate.

"Did you sleep well?" he asked, putting a hand on each of their shoulders as he walked by to fill a cup with coffee.

"I dreamed a prince carried me to bed," Mia said and giggled.

Shandra laughed. "A handsome prince did carry you to bed." She placed a kiss on his cheek.

"Sheba is too cuddly. She kept pushing me out of bed," Jayden said, petting the dog's head.

"Maybe we should make her sleep on the floor," Ryan said.

"No!" both children said in unison and Sheba woofed.

Shandra laughed. "I think it's unanimous that Sheba will remain on the bed for a bit longer. But she'll have to go back to sleeping on the floor soon. Because I'm going to buy you bunk beds."

They both frowned.

"You don't like bunkbeds?" Ryan asked.

"We both like to sleep up top," Mia said.

"I can get you two tall beds. But if you sleep up high, Sheba will definitely be sleeping on the floor." Shandra set plates of four-inch round pancakes with smiles and eyes out of chocolate chips in front of the two.

"Wow!" Jayden said, poking at an eye with his finger.

"Chocolate in a pancake! I've never had chocolate in a pancake!" Mia started to pick the pancake up with her fingers.

"Fork," Ryan said.

She glanced at him, grinned, and picked up her fork. "Daddy always told me to use my fork. Mommy didn't care. She said it was less to wash if I ate with my hands." The corners of her mouth started to droop.

"Here, sprinkle a few little ones on there and it tastes like a warm chocolate chip cookie," Shandra said, distracting the girl.

Once there were miniature chips sprinkled over the pancake, Shandra used a knife and fork, cutting the pancake into bite-sized pieces.

Ryan walked over to the platter of pancakes and dug out several without chocolate and added the egg Shandra had fried. He sat back down next to Jayden and prepared his pancakes with butter and syrup the way he liked them.

"Why don't you like sleeping on the bottom bunk?" Ryan asked casually. He had other questions for Jayden but thought he'd start with this one.

The boy acted as if the bite he was swallowing became stuck. He picked up the glass of milk in front of his plate and drank half the liquid before putting the cup down and poking at a piece of pancake with his fork. "If we slept on the bottom, sometimes Mommy would come in during the night and lay with us. She'd talk about scary things and then we couldn't sleep. In the morning Daddy would ask us if we were sick. Mommy didn't want us telling him she came in and visited us so we'd say we were. He'd tell Mommy to take us to the doctor. But she'd go to town and leave us home then give Daddy the bill from the doctor. When we both slept on the top, she'd still lay down on the bottom and talk, but we'd pull the covers over our heads and not hear her as much."

Mia nodded. "She'd say things like a man from the prison would come get us and a dragon lady would breath fire and cook us for dinner." She shuddered.

"Well, I can guarantee no one will come tell you bad stories. I'll get you each a twin-size bed and you can each have your own side of the room." Shandra said.

"What about Sheba?" Mia asked, patting the dog's head with sticky fingers, spiking the fluffy black fur.

"She can sleep on one person's bed one night and the other person's bed the next night until you are both comfortable sleeping alone." Shandra sat down with a plate of pancakes.

Ryan's phone buzzed. Forensics. "I'll see you all tonight." He kissed the top of Shandra's head and patted the children on the head, before walking into the dining room to retrieve his computer.

"What do you have?" he asked after the tech announced who he was.

"The fatal shot came from the shotgun you sent us. It was a definite match. There weren't any prints on the shotgun, it had been wiped. But there was a fresh scratch on the wood stock. Not sure if it pertains to your homicide or not, but we are analyzing it."

"Anything else I sent you from that scene stick out as odd?" Ryan asked.

"No. But the other crime scene…I'm pretty sure you can rule it a homicide as well. That blade you sent still had traces of aconitum napellus or monkshood. It's a toxic plant that grows everywhere. The poison can be absorbed through the skin. In this case, it was absorbed into the bloodstream through the slitting of the wrists."

"Does it cause vomiting?" Ryan thought about the earlier report.

"Yes. From what I pulled from the blade, there was more than a lethal dose on it. Besides vomiting, the victim would have been awake through all the effects but paralyzed and unable to do anything."

Ryan rubbed a hand over his eyes. "How long would that have been?"

"Anywhere from ten minutes to I'd say not more than an hour."

His first concern was whether or not Jayden had come back to the house when his mother was in the last stages. Had he cleaned up the vomit, thinking she'd taken drugs?

"Thanks. Anything else?"

"There were traces of gun powder on both victim's clothing."

Chapter Sixteen

Lil and the children were feeding the horses as Shandra drove down her driveway headed to town to get schoolwork for the twins. She had a feeling they were behind after hearing how their mom had manipulated them to get a chance to see the doctor. She'd asked the kids if they knew the name of the doctor. They didn't know the name but it was a big house in Warner.

She'd told Lil not to expect her back until midafternoon. She planned to purchase beds in Warner after picking up the schoolwork.

Entering Huckleberry, Shandra turned left following the signs to the school. She'd only been to the school once before. Remembering the event, chilled her blood. Ryan's mom had asked Shandra to have Sheba pull a sleigh full of toys in the Christmas parade. The parade ended at the school for a Christmas fundraising event. Sheba had bolted when the car ahead of her backfired. When Shandra found the scared dog, Sheba had been stabbed and a body was in the sleigh. And that had been the beginning of a murder investigation to save Ryan's life.

She pulled into the school's visitor parking area and walked up to the old school that she was pretty sure had housed all twelve grades when it was first built. Now the Huckleberry high schoolers were bused to Warner High.

The sound of children at recess made her smile. She wondered if Mia and Jayden had friends they'd like to play with. She'd ask their teacher. Inside the building, she spotted a sign that said, OFFICE, Visitors Check In.

She walked up to the office window and smiled at the young woman sitting at a desk.

"Hello." The woman rose and hurried to the window. "What can I help you with?"

"I'm Shandra Greer. My husband and I are taking care of Mia and Jayden Woodcock—"

"Weren't Mitch and Jessica's deaths terrible? How are the twins? We've been wondering about them." The woman appeared to genuinely care.

"They are doing as well as can be expected. I was hoping to speak with their teacher and get some work so they can stay caught up until my husband believes they should come back to school." She heard a chair creak in a room down a small hallway beyond the secretary's desk.

"When do you think they will be returning?" the secretary asked.

"We don't know. Is there a chance I could speak

with their teacher?"

A short, thin woman with gray hair walked up to the window. "I'm Mrs. Trindel, the principal. I overheard that you have Mia and Jayden. Dear children. How are they holding up?"

"As well as can be expected," Shandra repeated herself. "I would like to speak with their teacher and get their schoolwork."

"Yes, of course." Mrs. Trindel turned to the secretary. "I'll take Mrs…" she faced Shandra. "I'm sorry I missed your name."

"Greer. Mrs. Greer."

The woman nodded. "I'll take Mrs. Greer down to Mrs. Couch's room. They can visit, and I'll keep an eye on the class. Take messages for any calls that come in." The small woman stepped out of the office and started down the hall. "Follow me."

Shandra was surprised at how fast the woman's short legs carried her down the hall. She stopped at the door of a room with a big Teddy bear poster holding a sign that said Mrs. Couch.

"I'll go in and have her come out here to talk to you." The woman opened the door and disappeared, leaving Shandra standing in the hall.

She remembered standing in lines in a hallway much like this as a child. Waiting to go into the room after recess, waiting to go to the cafeteria for lunch. Waiting to get on the bus. She'd hated the long bus ride to and from school. She couldn't wait to turn sixteen and drive herself back and forth. Granted it had been a beater truck that she'd been able to buy with her own money, but Adam couldn't take the pickup from her. It was hers.

The door opened. "Mrs. Greer, I'm so glad you came. I've been worried sick about Mia and Jayden." The woman who stepped out the door was in her thirties, a tall, robust woman with a pleasant smile.

"Is there some place we can talk? I'd like to ask you some questions as well as get their schoolwork," Shandra said, scanning the hallway for a place to sit.

"We'll go in the teacher's lounge. There shouldn't be anyone there this time of day."

She followed the woman down the hall a short distance. The woman's skirt swayed as her ample hips moved up and down when she walked.

"In here."

Shandra entered a brightly lit room with three conference type tables in a U-shape.

"We have coffee, water, or pop. Or I can microwave some water for tea if you'd like." Mrs. Couch stood by a small kitchenette.

"I'm fine." Shandra sat and waited for the woman to sit in the chair across from her. "I have so many questions. What kind of students are they? Are they at grade level? Do they have friends they might want to play with? Were their parents active in their education?"

Mrs. Couch raised her hands. "You sound as if you plan to keep the children."

"That's up in the air at the moment. I only want to make them feel normal. Or as normal as they can considering both their parents are dead."

"Have you talked to the aunt? She was more hands-on with their education than their mother. Mitch came in for all the conferences, but I believe Mrs. Woodcock came in once when the children were in first grade."

"The aunt has been to the school checking on the twins?" Shandra wondered why she hadn't tried to see them if she was that close with them or that they hadn't mentioned her or staying with her.

"Yes, she's picked them up at least half a dozen times, saying her sister was busy. From what I know Mrs. Woodcock didn't have a job, so I'm not sure why she would be too busy to pick up her children." The scorn in the woman's voice told Shandra how much the teacher had thought of the twin's mother.

"I learned this morning that there were days they didn't go to school. Are they behind in their school work?" Shandra planned to work with them. They were both bright children who deserved to be up with their peers.

"They did tend to miss a lot of school. At least one day a week. They both try hard to keep up." Mrs. Couch peered into her eyes. "They could both have wonderful futures if someone cared enough."

Shandra nodded. "What about friends? Any in particular they might want to play with?"

Sadness filled the teacher's eyes. "They have always stayed to themselves. It was as if they didn't want to make friends."

"Ok. You've answered my questions. I'd like you to show me what they need to do for schoolwork, and I'll make sure when they come back they are caught up to the rest of the class." Shandra wouldn't allow the children to lose any more self-esteem. It appeared their mother had tried to keep them suppressed. And the father tried his best to keep them fed, clothed, and sheltered.

~*~

Ryan walked into the open rollup door of Webb Automotive Repair. The man the bartender pointed out as Ray, a Webb employee, stood by a toolbox rummaging through it.

"Excuse me?" Ryan said.

The man whirled around. He'd clearly been startled. "Who are you?"

Ryan flashed his badge. "Detective Greer, Weippe Sherriff's Department. I'd like to ask you some questions about Mitch Woodcock."

The man relaxed. "He was a good guy. Worked hard. Loved his kids."

Nodding, Ryan noticed he hadn't said loved his family or his wife. Just kids. "When was the last time you saw him?"

"Friday afternoon." The man slammed a drawer shut on the tool box. "Couldn't believe the boss fired him. We are up to our eyeballs in work and he fires the best mechanic."

"Did Mitch do something wrong to get fired?" Ryan pulled his notepad out of his pocket.

"Not workwise, but I think he and the boss's wife might have been…" He made a fist and his arm moved back and forth like a piston. "You know what I mean."

"I think I do. Any idea how long that was going on?"

The man glanced toward what appeared to be a small office in the corner. "Longer than the boss knew."

Ryan smiled. "You knew but the boss didn't?"

The man grinned back, "Yeah. Mrs. Webb would come by days the boss was out of town picking up parts. The two, Mitch and her, would go in the office and not come out for a bit. She'd have grease on her when she'd come out."

"You think the boss would do more than fire Mitch, knowing he was fooling around with his wife?"

Ray thought for several seconds, wiping the tool he held with a rag. "He has a temper. But are you asking if he killed Mitch…I think he would have killed Mrs. Webb before he did Mitch."

"Thanks." Ryan nodded toward the office. "Mr. Webb in?"

"Yeah."

"What's your last name Ray?"

"Little."

Ryan jotted the man's full name in his notepad and walked over to the office. He knocked and walked in.

Webb was on the phone. He scowled and continued talking. "Yeah, I need three belts added to yesterday's order." He rattled off numbers and hung up the phone. "Can I help you?"

Ryan showed his badge and stated who he was. "I'd like to know why you fired Mitch Woodcock last Friday?"

Webb's face reddened and his lips pinched together before he exploded. "What does that have to do with anything?"

"He was fired Friday and shot to death on Saturday. Your firing him could have an impact on who killed him." Ryan held his pen over the notepad, waiting.

The eyes staring at him vibrated. No doubt he was trying to come up with a good response. "He screwed up on a brake job. A lady could have been hurt."

"The name of the woman?"

"Why do you need to know that?" Webb's right leg

was bouncing.

"To follow up and make sure that family didn't retaliate about the bad brake job. I have to follow all the leads. A man and his wife were killed."

"Jessica didn't kill herself?" Relief eased the anger that had been on his face.

"No, I'm working two homicide cases. Husband and wife. Why did you fire Mitch?" Ryan wasn't leaving until he had the answer the employee suspected.

"Good to know Jessica didn't, you know. I thought she did it because I fired Mitch." Webb seemed to have taken the woman's death harder than his employee's.

"Mitch was killed first. Then Jessica. Any idea who would want to kill both of them?" Ryan studied the man.

His brow furrowed as he thought.

"Other than you?" Ryan said, quietly.

"Why would I want to kill them?" This riled the man back up.

"Because Mitch was fooling around with your wife and maybe Jessica was going to blackmail you?" Ryan was grasping at anything to make the man talk. He did realize that Jessica seemed to be only interested in herself. If Mitch were fired, and she didn't have money for her habit, she'd have to find it elsewhere. But then why did she have a box of meth hidden?

"You don't know what the hell you're talking about!" Webb shouted so loud Ryan bet everyone within a block heard him.

"Do you mean Jessica blackmailing you or the fact Mitch and your wife were having an affair?" Ryan ducked when the man threw a punch. He dropped the notepad, grabbed the man's arms behind his back, and cuffed him. "You just assaulted an officer. It looks like the best place to question you is the police station."

Ryan hauled Webb through the repair shop. Webb shouted to Ray to call his wife and tell her to get down to the police station.

Shoving the man in the back of his SUV, Ryan wondered why Webb requested his wife come to the station. Maybe to call a lawyer?

Chapter Seventeen

Shandra stood in front of a large older house in Warner. The sign out front said Dr. Murphy's, hours were 10:00 am – 4:00 pm, Monday- Friday. He or she was obviously a doctor that worked limited hours.

Entering the door with the Open sign, Shandra was surprised by the entryway. It had three chairs, a small area with toys, and a split door, with the top half open, into a room to the right.

"Good morning." A young male receptionist stepped up to the split door. "We don't take calls from pharmaceutical reps any day but Tuesday."

"I'm not a pharmaceutical rep." Shandra faced the young man.

"We don't take new patients on any day but Thursday." He pointed to a sign on the wall beside the doorway.

"I'm not here as a patient. I'd like to speak to the

doctor about patients, Jayden and Mia Woodcock. My husband and I are fostering them until things are settled.”

The young man tipped his head. “They finally took the children away from Jessica?”

“No, Jessica and Mitch are dead. Why would they take the children away?” Shandra wondered at this receptionist knowing something that Children’s Services should have known.

An older woman walked out of a room down the hall. She smiled at Shandra and waved at the receptionist. “See you next week.”

When the woman had closed the door behind her, the receptionist opened the bottom half of the door and walked down the hall, knocking on the door the older woman had appeared from.

He opened the door, spoke briefly, and waved Shandra toward him. “Dr. Murphy will see you. She has fifteen minutes before her next patient.”

Shandra walked in the room, expecting to see an older woman. What she discovered was a woman with short, spiky hair, dyed rainbow colors with large glittery glasses. She looked like a rocker from the 80s in a white doctor’s coat.

“Gil says you have the Woodcock children. Do you live in Warner?” The woman was abrupt.

Shandra held her hand out to the doctor. “I’m Shandra Greer. My husband and I are fostering the twins.”

The doctor shook hands and that’s when Shandra noticed the scarring on her hand and lower arm.

“We don’t live in Warner. My husband is a detective with the sheriff’s department.” Shandra sat in the chair in front of the woman's desk.

"What do you want to know from me?"

"You are the children's doctor, correct?" Shandra didn't miss the hesitancy before the woman nodded.

"Yes. They don't have any allergies, unusual this day and age, and considering their mother's addictions."

This was what Shandra wanted to know about. "Why did Jessica come see you almost once a week? Did you know she would keep the children up all night before so she could come see you and tell her husband she brought the children here?"

The doctor leaned back in her chair. "She was trying to kick her addiction. I counseled her and gave her medication for depression. That's a usual side effect of quitting meth."

"And her husband didn't know this?" Shandra thought it odd a woman would keep her trying to get clean away from her husband.

Dr. Murphy shrugged. "I thought he did. The bill was always paid promptly and she was always on time for her appointments."

"When you saw the children, did you notice if their mother's condition was affecting them?" Shandra hadn't had much interaction with people who were addicted. Or if she did, she hadn't known. But there had to be some issues the children were going to face knowing she was a drug addict. Even if they were only seven.

"Jayden always asked me if he could do something to help his mother. I told him just love her and help her when she was struggling. I believe Mia knew something was wrong, but she didn't want to know about it. She's a more 'if you ignore it, it will go away' type." Doctor Murphy spun her chair and pulled out two files. She spread them on her desk. "They are both healthy though a bit thin. They could use more food. They are intelligent. Jayden has had one broken bone. He fell off the top bunk last year. Mitch brought him in." She raised a hand. "Before you ask, it was a typical break from a fall like that."

Shandra breathed a sigh of relief. They hadn't acted like they'd been physically abused, but she could tell they had emotionally. "Thank you, Dr. Murphy. This will be a big help as we get to know these two and help them."

~*~

The Huckleberry Police Station interview room was small and stuffy. Ryan sat across from Webb waiting for him to cooperate.

The man refused to say anything until his wife arrived.

"Ryan, Mrs. Webb is here," Blane, the youngest member of the Huckleberry Police force, and the most zealous, opened the door. He'd tried to arrest Shandra for murder the first time they'd met.

"Send her in." Ryan stood, moving a chair over next to Webb.

Mrs. Webb walked in. Her eyebrows rose at the sight of him.

"Have a seat Mrs. Webb. Your husband wouldn't talk to me until you arrived." Ryan motioned to the chair he'd placed next to her husband.

She grasped the chair, pulling it to the end before sitting. The woman glanced briefly at her husband.

"Why would he want me here?"

He pointed to Webb. "You'll have to ask him."

"I want to talk to her alone," Webb said.

Mrs. Webb's head started vibrating back and forth. "I don't want to be in here alone with you."

Ryan crossed his arms. "Pretend I'm not in here. I'll just make sure you are civil to one another. Then I want my questions answered."

Webb glared at him. "I can't talk to her with you in the room."

"Why? Because you are going to tell her you weren't hunting or fishing or whatever you told her you were doing Saturday? Instead you followed her to the cabin. When she left and you went in to confront Mitch, you found him dead, and you think she did it?"

Both their necks cracked as their heads spun and they stared at one another.

"By the way, Jayden confirms the time you said you were at the cabin," Ryan said to Mrs. Webb.

"You've already talked to him?" Webb shouted. The man didn't seem to have any other volume.

"I visited with your wife yesterday, but I couldn't seem to catch up to you." Ryan pushed a photo of Mitch with a hole the size of a softball torn just below his rib cage across the table. "Is that what you saw? Or did you visit him before your wife? Did you shoot him, then circle back hoping to arrive right behind your wife so you would have an alibi?"

Webb shoved the photo away. "I didn't do that. I fired him. And I told him if he didn't stay away from my wife, I'd make sure he'd not be able to find work within a hundred miles of here."

"I was going to see him to tell him I was sorry you fired him and I'd help him find a new job. I was the reason you fired him. You're always saying he's the best mechanic in all of Weippe County." Mrs. Webb glared at her husband. "You don't want me. You stay at the bars until they close then leave in the morning before I get up. Why would you care that someone was paying attention to me?"

"I stay at the bars because I can't stand the way you look at me."

"Why don't you just get a divorce or separate? It's obvious you are both unhappy," Ryan said, then wished he'd kept that thought to himself.

"I kept asking Mitch to leave Jessica, then I would have divorced Richard, but he said he couldn't. He didn't love her. Said he never had. I think her getting pregnant was a mistake and he did the noble thing and married her. Only he didn't realize how horrible her addiction was." Mrs. Webb shook her head. "That woman didn't deserve those two beautiful children."

Ryan made a note that it seemed Mrs. Webb spent time with the twins. He'd ask them about it. He had another thought. "Do you know where the twins were born? In Warner or Huckleberry?"

"I think they were born in Washington. That's where Mitch was going to college." Mrs. Webb glared at her husband. "He may not have finished college, but he was more refined than you."

"Did Jessica follow him to college?" Ryan had thought neither one had made it out of Weippe County.

"No, she was working in Spokane helping Andie get through college. I guess she and Mitch met up there."

While his wife was talking, Webb sat in the chair brooding.

"You may both go." Ryan pointed a finger at Webb. "The next time I or any other cop wants to ask you questions, cooperate. It's much easier."

The man grunted.

Ryan stood and walked out of the room. He found the small space in the Huckleberry Police Station where there was a desk and computer for visiting Weippe County Sheriff's personnel and State Police to use rather than traveling to their stations. He wanted to find out when Mitch attended college and learn what he could about Jessica while she was in Spokane.

Chapter Eighteen

"Whew! I'm glad you two are so strong," Shandra said, sitting on one of the twin beds, she, the twins, and Lil put in the guest bedroom.

"I like my sheets," Mia said, pulling the set of unicorn sheets out of the packaging.

"I'm glad you like them. I haven't known you for very long, but I thought every girl liked unicorns." Shandra picked up the plastic wrap, watching Jayden carefully unwrap the Superhero cartoon character sheets she'd bought for him. "And you," she ruffled Jayden's hair. "I have no idea what you like. The toys Ryan brought home last night and your clothes didn't really tell me much."

A smile spread across Jayden's face. "These are great! Daddy and I watched a Spiderman movie once. He's right there." He pointed to the web-slinging crime fighter.

"I can take them back and get you Spiderman sheets," Shandra offered.

"No. I want to learn about all of these heroes."

Lil grabbed the sheets out of the kids' hands. "They have to be washed before you can put them on the beds. They put too many chemicals in stuff these days." She stomped off to the laundry room.

The twins still held their hands as if they were holding invisible sheets, staring at the door.

"Looks like Lil knows more about this stuff than I do." She clapped her hands as if bringing them out of a trance. "Want to go for a horseback ride with me?"

"Yeah!" they both shouted.

"Good. Because tomorrow we'll dig into your schoolwork."

"Ohhh. Do we have to?" Jayden whined as they all three walked to the back door.

"Yes. We're going to get you both caught up and feeling good about school." Shandra popped her head into the Laundry room. "Would you like to go riding with us?"

Lil closed the washing machine lid. "You planning on putting the two of them on Oliver?"

"Yes. You could ride Duke or Sammy." Shandra knew Lil would be sad for a while when they rode. She'd spent a lot of years on Sunshine's back, riding this mountain.

"I think I'll come along. Wouldn't mind seein' those two kid's faces light up."

~*~

Ryan called the admissions office at Gonzaga and after waiting through several different office receptionists, discovered that Mitch had gone to

Gonzaga on a football scholarship. He'd played that fall, drank too much at a party toward the end of the season, and ended up with an injury that put him out of the program and out of college unless he paid for it himself.

On a whim he asked the person on the other end of the conversation. "Could you look up Andie…" He thumbed through the reports for Jessica's last name.

"Woodcock? She's listed as Mitch's wife. She attended all four years getting a degree in Computer Science. She is now listed on our alumni list as Andie Teague. I assume she remarried."

Ryan sat back in his chair. "Thank you." The younger sister had been married to Mitch before the older sister. Since no one knew, they must have married in Washington and divorced there. He wanted to know the dates. If the college was in Spokane most likely their marriage certificate should be there too.

Looking up the year Mitch entered college in the Spokane public records, he discovered that Mitch and Andie were married from the month they entered college until July the following year. Basically, ten months.

On a whim, he looked up the marriage license for Mitch and Jessica. They married the month after Mitch and Andie split. He did the math. The twins were born in June before the divorce. Had Jessica become pregnant from Mitch while he was married to Andie? That would make Andie hate her sister and be bitter toward Mitch. But enough to kill both of them? And leave her niece and nephew orphans?

He did a search of births in June in Spokane. Bingo! Twins to Mitch and Andie Woodcock. Andie was their biological mother. That was why Jessica had said his brat kids. Why had she taken on the role of the children's mother if she wasn't? Why had Mitch and Andie divorced?

There was only one way to find out. He glanced at his watch. He wasn't going to make dinner tonight either. He hoped Shandra would forgive him for talking her into fostering, then never being home.

Ryan jotted down all he'd learned and headed out to his vehicle. Sitting in the driver's seat, he pulled out his phone, and dialed Shandra. He waited for her voicemail message to finish and said, "I'm not going to make dinner tonight. I learned something that might be good news for the kids. I'll tell you when I get home."

On the drive to Warner and the Teague residence, he had Cathleen on speakerphone. "Did you ever learn anything more about Andie Teague and her husband?"

"She works from home for a large computer corporation and her husband works for a commercial insurance agency. They married in college. No children. However, they have been going to a fertility doctor and word from there is she had a miscarriage a couple weeks ago."

"No mention of her first marriage in anything you looked up?"

"First marriage? I didn't see anything. Where did you see that?" Cathleen's tone held interest.

"Spokane marriage licenses. That's why I'm going to talk to her."

"Want me to bring the kids by this weekend to play with the two you have?" Cathleen asked.

"Let's give them a little more settling in time. Maybe after we figure out who killed their parents."

Ryan didn't mind his nieces and nephews being role models for the twins, but they were still unstable at this point.

"Sounds good. Maybe when you make an arrest, we can have a family gathering at Mom and Dad's."

"Talk to Shandra, but I'm sure that will work. Gotta go. Thanks for the information." Ryan parked behind a new model Lexus. The couple had money. Had Andie ditched Mitch when he wouldn't be able to play football and pay for his education?

Walking up to the door, he was once again impressed with the place and wondered why, if the twins were hers, Andie hadn't claimed them.

He knocked on the door and waited.

Heavy footsteps. Teague was answering the door. He doubted he'd get much out of Andie with her husband around, considering she hadn't told him about her father being in prison.

"Detective Greer," Teague backed up after seeing who was at the door. "Come in. I'd love to learn more about my wife and you seem to know more than I do."

Ryan smiled and moved by him. "I have some questions for you, too. Is your wife home?"

"Yes. She's been in bed since your last visit. Which means I've been working from home."

Yet he was still dressed in fancy slacks, a button-up shirt, but no tie.

The man led him into the dining room. "Would you like a cup of coffee?"

"Thanks." Ryan took the seat the man waved a hand toward.

Teague walked through the door between the dining room and kitchen. There was a wide opening above a counter between the two rooms. He watched as the man deftly poured two cups of coffee, placing them on a tray along with a sugar bowl and a pitcher he'd filled with creamer from the refrigerator.

Back in the dining room, Teague placed a cup in front of Ryan and the sugar and cream in the middle of the table between the two of them. He sat down. "What did you wish to ask me?"

Ryan sipped the coffee. It tasted a lot like the dark roast the Aducci's served at their restaurant in Huckleberry. "This is good. Where did you meet your wife?" He pulled out his notepad.

Teague stopped with the creamer suspended over his coffee cup. "What does that have to do with my sister-in-law's death?"

Ryan shrugged. "Probably nothing, but I like to know everything about the people close to the victims."

"I see. Profile the family to get a better idea about the victim."

Ryan nodded, if that's what the man wanted to think, so be it.

"Jessica was the total opposite of Andie. You've met my wife. She's refined, a lady. Until the other night I would have never guessed her father was in prison. Can you tell me what he did?"

Ryan had been studying the man as he talked. It appeared he was going to use this time to find out answers himself. "I think that would be something you should ask your wife."

"She just cries every time I ask her." The man frowned.

"Then maybe you should find a more subtle way to bring up the subject. When did you and Andie meet?"

"In college. Gonzaga in Spokane. I played basketball. She was and still is gorgeous. I could tell she carried herself like a woman I wanted to marry. She was innocent and bright."

"Was that your freshman years?" Ryan knew it couldn't have been. Andie would have been pregnant with her then husband's children.

"No. My fourth year and her third year. She came to a frat party with her roommate. I could tell when she walked in that she'd never been to a frat house or a party the likes we put on back then." He smiled, reminiscing.

"Roommate. She wasn't living with her sister then?"

"No. Jessica had followed her and roomed with Andie her first year of college then when she realized Andie could make it on her own, she came back here. She, Mitch, and the kids."

"Do you remember who her roommate was?" Ryan wondered if this person knew the truth behind the sisters.

"No. We met the last term of my fourth year and married that fall. Then we lived off campus in the summer house behind my parents' home in Spokane."

Ryan was beginning to wonder if Andie divorced Mitch to find a catch like Teague. "And your parents got along with Andie and Jessica?"

Teague frowned. "They've never met Jessica. Andie wanted it that way."

"She didn't want your family to meet the person who helped her finish high school and get to college? That sounds a bit snobbish to me?" Ryan studied the man.

"Snobbish? Jessica was a loser and she married a loser. I preferred Andie didn't have them around. Who knew what her sister would do to score another hit?" The hatred on his face gave Ryan a moment to wonder if he had taken care of the rubbish in his wife's family.

"Could you go see if your wife would be willing to speak to me?" Ryan wanted answers. He couldn't get them talking to this pompous windbag.

Chapter Nineteen

The kids sat at the counter eating hot dogs and macaroni and cheese. They hadn't stopped talking since returning from the horseback ride. Shandra smiled, enjoying the banter between the two.

She'd been sorry Ryan wouldn't be home for dinner. She'd listened to his message as soon as they were low enough on the mountain her phone dinged. He would have enjoyed hearing about the ride.

"I think that girl deer was pretty," Mia said, loading her fork with macaroni and cheese.

"The boy was prettier. His horns—"

"Antlers," Shandra corrected him.

"Antlers were awesome. He had a head full of swords." Jayden said, wielding his fork like a sword.

"They fight with their antlers. In the fall, when they are rutting, they fight over the girl deer. You can hear the antlers clanking together." Shandra's heart expanded with the wonder in both the children's eyes.

"Will we be able to hear that?" Jayden asked.

"If you're still here."

The happiness vanished from them both.

"I want to stay here," Mia said. "I like Sheba, Lil, and you and Ryan."

Shandra walked up between them and put an arm around both their shoulders. "We'll have to see what happens after Ryan finds the person responsible for your parents' deaths and what your grandparents say."

Mia put a small arm around Shandra's waist and leaned her head against her ribs. "And Aunt Andie. What if she wants us? Do we have to go with her?"

Shandra studied the top of the child's head. Jayden was watching her. "Why wouldn't you want to go live with your aunt?"

"She cries a lot and Uncle Bradley doesn't like messes." Mia moved her head, gazing up at her. "They would never let us have a dog or horses."

"But they are family," Shandra said, making eye contact with both children.

"They don't feel like it," Jayden said, pulling out of her one-armed embrace and playing with his hotdog with his fork.

"Finish up. I have ice cream for dessert." Shandra wondered what Ryan was discovering.

~*~

Ryan entered the dark bedroom. Andie had insisted he come in the room and Bradley stay out.

"Mrs. Teague, I have some questions for you." Ryan snagged a chair by what looked like a woman's make-up dresser and set it several feet from the head of the bed where the woman sat propped up by pillows.

136

He sat and asked, "How are you feeling? Did your husband do anything to hurt you?"

"No! Bradley would never hurt me. I've had a migraine ever since you were here last. I'm sorry it's so dark but it's the only way I can stand sitting up and talking to you." Her voice was weak.

"Do you have these often?" he asked, wondering if this woman would be any better mother than her sister had been.

"Only when I'm stressed. My sister's death. Mitch…gone. I don't know if Bradley told you but I miscarried our child twelve days ago. This is all…too much." She sniffed and pulled a tissue from a box.

"I'm sorry, but I need to discover who killed your sister and brother-in-law so the children can be settled somewhere safe."

"What do you mean settled somewhere safe? Aren't they safe where they are now?" She leaned forward.

"They are safe where they are, but I've my suspicions Jayden knows something and whoever killed Jessica and Mitch may figure that out before I can find them." He tossed that out there to see how much motherly instincts she had for the twins.

"That's terrible! You really think he knows something?" She was searching rather than being concerned.

"I was wondering if you could tell me why you married Mitch in September of your first year of college and divorced him ten months later and never told anyone about the marriage or that the twins are yours?"

A moan so full of pain, it made his hair stand on

end, filled the room.

The door burst open. "What's wrong? Andie?" Teague closed the distance between the door and the bed in three strides. "What did you say to her?" The man faced Ryan.

He couldn't see Teague's expression as his back was to the open door and the light that streamed in. But his voice was full of rage.

"I asked her a simple question."

"Bradley, please. I'll be fine. Bring me another cup of my tea," Andie said in a weak voice.

"Are you sure you want me to leave you alone with him?" Teague wasn't budging.

"Please, I cried out because of a sharp pain."

Teague grasped her hand, before he left the room, closing the door gently.

"How long have you had these migraines?" Ryan asked.

"They started when I was pregnant. But Bradley knows nothing of my previous marriage or the twins. He would have never married me if he'd known I'd spent nine months as Mitch's wife." She leaned forward. "Please, don't tell him."

"He couldn't tell you'd had babies?" Ryan pondered that. From conversations, he'd overheard between his mom and sisters, there was no way a man couldn't tell a woman had birthed two children.

"I had a c-section. I told Bradley it was an operation for a burst appendix." She tilted her head, listening.

"He didn't know the scar was in an odd place for an appendectomy?" He was beginning to think Teague was a fool.

"You know men. They believe what they want to believe about a woman they want." She sunk back against the pillows.

"Why did you divorce Mitch and give him and your sister the twins?" It was evident the older sister had been unstable for some time.

"Mitch wouldn't give me a divorce unless I gave him the kids. He realized I'd only married him thinking he'd be making lots of money as a football player. When he ruined that by injuring himself, I wanted out of the marriage. But he discovered I was pregnant and made sure I carried to term. He wanted the kids. Jessica wanted the money she knew I'd pay to keep her quiet about me being the mother of the twins." This was spit out with as much venom as a rattlesnake.

"Did Mitch know she was blackmailing you?" Ryan asked as footsteps approached down the hall.

"No. He wouldn't have allowed it if he'd known."

"Why didn't you tell him?"

The door opened.

"Tell me what?" Teague asked, carrying a tray with a teapot, a cup, and saucer.

Ryan decided to wait and see what the woman said. No sense losing her confidence.

"That Jessica was blackmailing me to keep quiet about our father being in prison." Andie poured a small amount of the tea into her cup. She sniffed then sipped. "Not ready yet." Placing the cup on the tray with a shaky hand, it clattered.

"I knew she must have had something. You are strong enough to tell her no when she wanted money for a fix." Teague sat on the bed beside his wife. "Why didn't you tell me?"

"I knew how you wanted a pristine wife. But I loved you and didn't want to lose you if you found out about my father." She snuggled her head against his chest.

Ryan sat in the dark watching the two hold one another. It was an intimate moment. The awkwardness made him clear his throat.

"Detective, I'm sure you have nothing more to ask my wife." Teague continued to hold the woman, but Ryan could see by the silhouette of his face, the man was staring at him.

"I'm sorry, but I do have a few more questions."

"I'll be fine, Bradley. The tea will help. You go back to work. I've been holding you up enough the last few days." The woman sounded sincere and apologetic all at the same time.

"You're sure?" Teague asked.

"Yes. Go. I know you are working on something big." She kissed his cheek and he rose.

"I'll be in the office if you need anything." He walked out, closing the door quietly.

She poured tea into the cup and sipped, leaning back on the pillows.

"Why didn't you tell Mitch about Jessica blackmailing you?" Ryan asked, again.

She let out a breath. "Because as much as I hated it, I didn't want to get Jess in trouble. If it wasn't for her, I wouldn't have the career and husband I do. I felt I owed her for the years our father molested her and left me alone. For the years she worked constantly so I could have the life she never would. And for the years she put up with Mitch and my kids."

Ryan knew their father had gone to prison for

raping and eventually murdering one of his rape victims. How had Jessica felt knowing her father had started with her? Now he understood the woman so much better and had more compassion for her. Even though she'd been given a crappy life, she'd helped her sister out of the pit she herself had fallen into. But it appeared she hadn't realized what taking care of two children would be like and fell to drugs.

"Don't you even care about your children?" he asked.

She waved a hand. "I don't feel like they're mine. That's what I wanted. Little to no connection with them. It was a mistake that I don't want to ruin the rest of my life."

"You don't think your husband would embrace them even as your niece and nephew if you took them in?"

"He only wants a child we train to our way of life. He doesn't tolerate messes."

"I understand you've been going to a fertility doctor. Wouldn't it be simpler to admit the twins are yours and you could save money?" He didn't understand her not wanting her own children.

"Bradley wants a true Teague. One with his DNA."

Shaking his head, Ryan asked, "Where were you Saturday around noon?"

"Saturday? This past Saturday?" She was stalling.

"Yes, around noon." He waited for her to either remember or come up with something.

"I was here. Alone. I believe Bradley had gone golfing. Why do you want to know where I was on Saturday at noon?"

"You don't have anyone who can verify you were

here?”

“No. Do I need someone to?”

“And you don’t remember getting a call from your sister on Sunday, maybe complaining that Mitch had been killed and she wasn’t going to take care of your brats anymore?”

“No. I told you before, I didn’t get a call from Jessica on Saturday or Sunday.” She placed the tea cup on the bedside table. “You need to go or this migraine is never going to ease.”

“Do you know what will happen to the twins if you or Mitch’s parents don’t take them in?”

“They’ll have a better life than they had with their dad and Jessica. Close the door when you leave.”

Ryan walked out of the bedroom trying to understand how the twins’ own mother didn’t want them, and didn’t care what happened to them. He’d only known the two for three days and he cared.

He walked into the office off the living room. “Mr. Teague, can you tell me where you were this past Saturday at noon?”

The man’s head swiveled on his neck as he peered at Ryan. “This past Saturday? I went golfing.”

Ryan pulled out his notepad. “Who with?”

He scoffed. “There’s no one around here I want to golf with. I just go out and hit eighteen holes to get fresh air.”

“And Sunday were you and your wife home all day?”

“Sunday? I guess we were doing what we do most Sundays. We have a late breakfast and then go about puttering doing different activities we each enjoy.”

“Which are?” Ryan wasn’t letting him off with

such an evasive answer.

"A late breakfast, read the paper, listen to music, go for a walk, work in the yard. The usual Sunday things." He stared at Ryan. "Are you trying to say either my wife or I killed Mitch and Jessica?"

"Have you ever been to Mitch's cabin on Huckleberry Mountain?" Ryan wasn't going to let the man change the path he was headed down.

"I think we were invited there once for a birthday party for the twins. Why?"

"Has your wife been there more than the one time?" Ryan asked.

"I doubt it. She would have no reason to go to that backwoods shack for any reason other than the birthday." Teague stood. "I think it's time you left."

Ryan let himself out of the house but not before wandering through the kitchen to see what kind of tea Andie was drinking. It appeared to be a homemade herbal tea. He slipped some in a small brown evidence envelope and left.

Chapter Twenty

After showers and a story, the two kids settled down to sleep in their new beds. Poor Sheba couldn't decide which bed to sleep on. Shandra settled it by saying, the dog would sleep on Mia's bed on the even days and Jayden's the odd days. The children agreed, and Sheba hopped onto Mia's bed when she patted the covers.

"Why do you think Ryan is so late?" Jayden asked as Shandra raised her hand to turn out the light.

"When he starts asking questions he goes until he can't think of another one to ask. He'll be home shortly and you can see him in the morning. Unless you'd like him to come in and say goodnight when he gets home?" She didn't want to sound too eager and have the children think it was what she wanted.

"I'd like that," Jayden said.

"Me, too," Mia added.

"Then I will tell him. Good night." Shandra turned out the light, left the door ajar, and walked into the kitchen to finish cleaning it up. Ryan had texted he'd gone to the office to drop off something for the lab and would be home after that an hour ago. That meant he'd be home in another hour.

She'd thought about letting the twins stay up but knew it was best, according to her mother-in-law and sisters-in-law, to keep children on a schedule. She doubted they had much of a schedule with a mother who took drugs and a father who was working to keep them together.

After cleaning up the kitchen, she made a cup of chamomile tea and settled on the couch, shuffling what little she knew around in her mind. Her head grew heavy and she slid down on the couch. A quick nap would be good.

A tornado picked Shandra up. She called to Ryan, but didn't see him. Grandmother's face appeared in the center. Her hand beckoned Shandra to her. Using swimming motions, Shandra made her way through the swirling air to the center where the air was calm. She floated beside Ella. "Why are we in the middle of a storm?"

People twirled by. A man paying too much attention to a young girl. Another girl sat in the corner watching. A dead woman. The man behind bars. A woman dying. Two young women. Then Jayden and Mia tumbled by. Shandra tried to reach out to them, but she couldn't grasp their hands. She tried to leave the calm center, but Grandmother held her in the middle.

"I don't understand? I don't understand?"

Her shoulder shook. "Shandra, I'm home." Ryan's

voice penetrated the dream.

She slowly drifted from the dream and opened her eyes. She stared into her husband's caring face. "I was dreaming."

"I thought so. You said you didn't understand. That's usually what you say when you've had a dream with your grandmother in it." Ryan sat on the couch beside her.

"There was a storm, like a tornado." She went on to describe what she'd seen.

"The man in jail was Jessica and Andie's father. I learned today he molested Jessica and went to jail when rape escalated to murder."

"That's awful! We can't tell Mia and Jayden any of that." Her heart wept for the two in her guest room. She was surprised they weren't a handful hearing how their lives had been so far.

"Hopefully, they don't learn it until they are old enough to process that they won't become like him."

"Speaking of the two. They requested you come in and say good-night when you came home." She smiled at the surprise on Ryan's face.

"Really? They said that, you aren't just saying that to make me feel good."

"They requested." She waved. "Go tell them good-night, and I'll dish us up some dessert."

"Sounds good." Ryan kissed her forehead and stood.

She watched him walk across the room and down the hall. He would make an amazing father. He loved kids. Standing, she headed to the kitchen to put some cookies on a plate.

Ryan returned to the kitchen a big goofy grin on

his face. "Jayden said he stayed awake just to say good-night to me. He knows I'm working hard."

"What about Mia?"

"She was asleep but when I put a hand on her shoulder, she smiled. Those two are great kids, I don't understand the adults in their lives." Ryan let out an exasperated sigh.

"Grab a glass of milk and follow me into the great room," Shandra said, balancing the cookie plate, napkins, and her reheated cup of tea.

When they were settled and both nibbling on cookies, she asked, "What did you learn today?"

Ryan finished off the cookie and swallowed some milk before he stared into her eyes. His eyes drooped from tiredness and sadness.

"I learned their mother is really Andie, Jessica's sister."

Shandra put down her tea cup. She wanted to stay awake for all of this. "Really? Why did Mitch and Jessica have the kids?"

Ryan told her all about the first marriage, Andie dumping Mitch when it looked like he'd no longer be rich, and Jessica using the kids as leverage to get money out of her sister.

"They should never hear all of this." Shandra didn't want the two to think they were never wanted by anyone.

"I agree. I have some more questions for Jayden in the morning. What did you do today? Besides buy twin beds." He picked up another cookie and bit it.

"I visited the doctor that Jessica was supposed to take the kids to. It seems she was trying to clean up. The doctor was seeing her and giving her medicine to help her with her depression." Shandra studied Ryan. "But I don't understand. If she was trying to quit, why did she hide a box of drugs worth a lot of money? How long was she taking it? Could she have killed Mitch then herself?"

"I'm still waiting to hear back from the lab whether or not the drugs we found can be connected to any others that have been sold or collected." Ryan finished off the last of his milk. "That's a good theory. Her killing Mitch and then herself. I've heard of meth addicts who become paranoid then after they do something while high regret it later. Both victims had gunpowder on their clothing. Which would make sense of your theory, but it makes me think whoever shot Mitch, wore the same clothes to kill Jessica."

"Like they had dressed to not be noticed, or wanted to make it seem like Jessica killed Mitch then killed herself?" Shandra held the tea cup in front of her mouth. "Who benefits from both Mitch and Jessica's deaths?"

"The only one at the top of my list is Andie. She doesn't want her husband to learn of her past, any of it. But I don't understand why she would meet Mitch at the cabin and then kill him? Especially, if she knew the kids were there." He snorted. "Not that she'd care about traumatizing those two. She has absolutely no maternal DNA in her."

Ryan sat up straight. "She has homemade herbal tea she drinks for migraines."

"Are you thinking she might have known about the poisonous plant used to kill her sister?" Shandra didn't want the twins to have a murderous family, but the sister made more sense than anyone else.

"Come on. We won't discover anything tonight. I should have several more reports waiting for me in the morning." Ryan took the tea cup from her and picked up his glass and the cookie plate. "I'll put Sheba out and be in."

Shandra yawned and said, "Thank you."

Ryan put the dirty dishes in the sink, walked to the guest room door, and whispered for Sheba. The dog slowly lowered herself off the bed and went out the back door. Ryan stood outside by the door, listening to the night time forest sounds. It reminded him of growing up on his family's farm. He'd enjoyed evenings and nights laying on his back, looking up at the stars and listening to the crickets, birds, and farm animals. Here the stars were bright in the dark sky. The moon cast shadows at the sides of the studio, barn, and house. A horse snorted, one stomped a foot. In the trees the sound of an owl telling another to stay away echoed through the silence. If he didn't work out of Warner, he'd give that house up in a heartbeat. But there were times it was nice to have his place there to crash when it was a hectic day and he was too tired to drive all the way here.

But this was the perfect place for kids to grow up. He smiled remembering how Jayden had said he'd waited for him and Mia smiled in her sleep at his touch.

Sheba bounded back to him. They entered the house and the dog plodded into the guest room and back up on Mia's bed.

Ryan checked both children one more time, then turned off the lights as he made his way to the great room. His bag with his laptop sat on the dining room table. Maybe a report came in. He wanted to find the killer of Jessica and Mitch and a suitable future for the kids.

Pulling out his laptop, he heard the shower go on. Shandra hadn't gone straight to bed. He'd just look at his emails and if nothing new came in, he'd close it up and go to bed.

There was an email from the lab tech about the gun powder. Ryan had asked where the powder had been found on the clothing. He opened the report and started reading. On both victims the gunpowder found on their clothes was on their left shoulders. As if the hand with the gunpowder had rested there. Ryan leaned back. The killer knew them. Why else would they put a hand on their shoulders? And in the case of Mitch, it would have been after he'd been shot. Had the killer also put a hand on Jessica's shoulder after she died and having cleaned up the vomit, or before, to get the woman to lie down?

Chapter Twenty-one

The children and Shandra were in the kitchen when Ryan entered the next morning. The small heads swiveled his direction with smiles on their faces.

"Good morning," he said to everyone and made his way to the coffeemaker.

"Good morning," Mia said. She had a bite of pancake on the end of her fork. "Did you come tell us good night?"

"I told you he did," Jayden said, scowling at his sister.

Mia made a face back at him. "But you don't always tell me the truth."

"It's for your own good," Jayden crossed his arms.

"Sometimes it's good for everyone to know about bad things. It will help them all to be careful in the future," Shandra said.

Ryan wondered if she was trying to cryptically tell

him to ask the questions of Jayden that he wanted to know. He glanced at Shandra. She was studying the children.

"What could be more bad than Mommy and Daddy are dead?" Mia asked.

Ryan decided to talk to the girl, then if the boy jumped in, he would be giving his information freely. He sat down next to Mia with his coffee. Shandra set a plate of pancakes and eggs in front of him. "Thank you."

She smiled, grabbed a plate of pancakes and sat down on the other side of Jayden.

"Mia, what do you know about how your Mom and Dad died?" Ryan spread butter on his pancake as if he were just making conversation.

"She doesn't know nothin'." Jayden said.

Mia elbowed her brother. "I know that there was a sound like a gun, and Jayden told me to stay where I was, and he went to the cabin to check on Daddy. I got scared standing there by myself so I started walking back."

"Did you make it all the way to the cabin?" Ryan asked.

"No. I saw something moving fast. It was brown and I thought it was a bear. So I ran back to where Jayden told me to stay." She poked at her pancake with a fork. "Do you think it was a bear that Daddy shot at and it killed him?"

"A bear didn't kill Daddy," Jayden said. He peered at Ryan over his sister's head. "I saw someone in a brown coat hurrying through the trees when I got to the cabin."

"Man or woman?" Ryan asked.

The boy shook his head. "I only saw their back. Brown coat, long like cowboys wear on movies."

"Long hair or short?"

"They had the hood up." The boy peered down at his plate. "I'm no help."

"You're a big help. That's more than we knew before. Did your Dad have the shotgun hung over the door or leaning against something when you left the cabin?"

"He always took it with us when we went walking, like we did that morning. I don't remember—"

"It was leaned against the wall by the door when we walked out." Mia smiled. "I remembered because I thought that meant Daddy was planning to go on another walk with us."

Ryan patted the girl's back. "This is all good to know. And when you returned home. How was your mom acting?"

"She wasn't there when Mrs. Webb took us home," Mia said. "We ate cereal and went to bed."

"When did she come home?" Ryan asked.

"In the morning. She must have seen our cereal bowls. She slammed the bedroom door open and yelled at us for being home." Mia's face became less animated, her eyes withdrawn.

"She was mad. She said we messed up her plans." Jayden frowned. "She was always saying we messed up her life. We tried to keep the house clean. We were worried about Daddy and forgot to put our things away."

Ryan knew the woman hadn't meant the house, but he kept his thought to himself. "You said she didn't believe you when you told her your dad was dead.

What did she say?"

"She said everyone loved Daddy. No one would kill him." Jayden made a face. "The way she said 'everyone' sounded mean."

Jessica knew about Mitch fooling around. She was still high on his suspect list for killing Mitch, but it didn't make sense if she hated the kids, hated her life, killing Mitch only gave her more responsibility. And why did she have gunpowder residue on her shoulder just like Mitch?

"You said she called your aunt and told you to leave the house?" Ryan didn't want to pull out his notepad to check what he'd written down.

"Yeah. She said she was going to call Aunt Andie." Jayden picked up his glass of milk. "She only called her when she wanted money."

"Maybe sisters aren't as close as brothers and sisters," Mia said, patting her brother's arm. The two stared at each other for nearly a minute.

Ryan wasn't sure whether to break in or not.

"More syrup?" Shandra asked, breaking the spell between the two children.

"Please," Mia licked her fork.

"You told me that you were out in the forest playing and thought your mom was sleeping when you came back to the house and you left her alone." Ryan needed to know who cleaned up the vomit. The child or the killer to make it look like a suicide. "Did you go in her room and try to help her?"

Jayden shook his head. "She never liked us around when she was in her room. It meant she wasn't feeling good. Daddy was the only one who could go in and check on her."

That answered his question. The killer had cleaned up what would have told them right away it had been poison and not suicide.

"As soon as you finish breakfast, you can sit down at the dining room table and we'll get you started on the school work you're missing," Shandra said.

The two children groaned, but continued shoveling in the pancakes.

Ryan finished eating, grabbed his laptop, and headed for the door. "See you all tonight." In his vehicle he wrote out warrants to search the Teague and Webb residences and vehicles as well as the Webb automotive shop. There had to be a brown coat with gunpowder on it at one or the other of those places. Unless the killer had already destroyed it. He also requested the phone records for the phone at the Woodcock residence. Mitch had a cell phone but Jessica didn't. At least not one that showed up on any paperwork.

~*~

Shandra sat at the table happily helping the two with their math when Lil entered through the back door and clumped down the hall.

"Wondered why these hooligans didn't come out to help me feed the horses." Lil sat down beside Mia. "Whatcha doin?"

"Math. I don't like numbers. They don't tell stories like words do." Mia had her left elbow on the table, her cheek rested in the palm of that hand while she scribbled on the math page with the pencil in her right hand.

"Sure, math tells a story. Show me your paper." Lil held out her hand.

Shandra watched as the child slid her workbook over in front of the woman.

Lil studied it for nearly a minute, then nodded. "Just as I thought. There is a story here."

Mia straightened and stared at the page. "Where?"

"Right here. You have twelve unicorns and you sell two of them to a circus. How many do you have left?" Lil glanced up from the page and studied Mia.

The girl thought, then held up her fingers and counted all ten, then two more to make twelve. "Ten! I have ten unicorns."

"Write it down." Lil's finger pointed to the equation.

Mia wrote down the number. "What about this one?" she asked, gazing at Lil with awe.

"Let's see. This one says twenty-three tigers escaped from the zoo. They joined thirteen tigers in the jungle. How many tigers are in the jungle?"

Mia started counting on her fingers.

"No, like this." Lil took her pencil and using the piece of paper Shandra gave each of the children for working out the problems, she wrote down the numbers and showed Mia how to work the problem while still talking about the tigers.

Jayden shook his head. "That just makes it harder."

Shandra leaned close to him. "You understand numbers better and your sister understands words better. This helps her, so let her and Lil have their fun."

He shrugged and pushed his workbook toward Shandra. All of the pages that needed to be done were. He'd whizzed right through the math work.

"Good job. You can go play outside with Sheba for ten minutes then you'll need to work on reading. But

you don't have to do all the work to catch up today."
She closed the math workbook.

"Come on Sheba," Jayden headed to the hall.

"What about me?" Mia asked.

"You finish that page and you can go, too."

The child smiled and turned her attention to the book and Lil, who was telling another story.

Shandra hadn't thought about Lil helping school the kids. It would be nice to have someone to keep them working if she needed to go somewhere in the morning. They needed to get caught up and feel confident when they went back to school. Wherever that may be.

She walked into the kitchen, set a timer on the stove, and watched Sheba and Jayden playing in front of the house. Running down the hall, the door slamming, and a delighted screech brought Mia into the scene outside the window.

"Those two are somethin'," Lil said behind her.

"Yes, they are." Shandra faced her friend. "They have bad dreams, but they don't act out and haven't drawn away from us."

"What's going to happen to them?" Concern warmed Lil's question.

"It depends on their aunt and grandparents." Even though Ryan had told her that Andie was the mother, the kids didn't know that and she didn't plan to say a thing. It was up to the woman to reveal that.

"You'd of thought they would have come here to at least see the two by now." Criticism dripped from Lil's words.

Shandra nodded. "Yeah. Who wouldn't want these two?"

Chapter Twenty-two

By the time Ryan pulled into the Weippe County Sheriff's Office, the search warrants for the Teague and Webb residences were ready. He grabbed Deputy Speaks and requested Deputy Trapp join them at the Teague residence in forty minutes.

"You want me to ride with you or take my own vehicle?" Speaks asked.

"Bring your own. We might have to split up." Ryan climbed back into his SUV and headed out of Warner towards Coeur d'Alene. The Teague's house was in one of the more prestigious home developments on the highway toward Coeur d'Alene. The trip from the development to Coeur d'Alene was a little over an hour. No different than commuting in the larger cities.

He pulled up to the house. There wasn't a car in the driveway, but there was a three-car garage. Speaks pulled in beside him and before they were out of their vehicles, Trapp pulled up behind the other patrol car.

The three of them approached the front door. Ryan rang the bell and they waited.

"Go around and see if someone may be in the backyard," he told Trapp.

Ryan rang the doorbell and knocked. He motioned to Speaks. "Check the garage for vehicles."

The deputy jogged over to the garage and down the side.

"Hey, what are you doing?" came a shout from the back of the house.

Ryan headed around the corner and discovered Trapp pulling Bradley Teague's arms behind his back.

"What's this about?" Ryan asked.

Teague was wiggling to get loose.

"He took a swing at me," Trapp said.

"I didn't know who he was," Teague said.

Trapp waved a hand down his body like a model. "I'm wearing a county uniform."

Teague's face reddened.

"Is your wife in the house?" Ryan asked.

"Yes, she's still not feeling well."

Trapp released the man.

Teague shook his arms and glared at the deputy.

Ryan handed him the warrant. "This is to search your house, cars, and land. Deputy Trapp will escort you in to tell your wife. You both need to wait out here on the patio while we search."

"The sunlight will make her headache worse." Teague stood his ground.

"Then I suggest you find a way to shade her better. Go get her and bring her out." Ryan motioned for Trapp to grab the man and take him in the house.

Speaks arrived. "Two cars in the garage."

"When Trapp gets the husband and wife out here, we'll start looking in the garage." Ryan studied the well-maintained yard. "Let's look around out here while we wait. The owner took a swing at Trapp. There must have been a reason he didn't want anyone seeing what he was doing."

They split up going different directions around the perimeter of the lot. In the back, behind a hedge, Ryan discovered a small garden of herbs and flowers. He took photos of all the plants.

"Over here!" Speaks called.

Ryan came out from behind the hedge and spotted Speaks, digging in what looked like an outdoor firepit.

"There's something besides wood been burned in this pit." Speaks had a piece of wood in his hand as he stirred the ashes in the pit. "These are still warm."

Ryan took photos of the short smoke tendrils and the ashes. "Spread it out so it will cool enough we can bag it." There was a scratching noise on the metal pit. "What was that?"

"The stick is dragging something." Speaks moved the stick to the edge and over.

Ryan picked up what dropped over the edge. A metal snap. They may have just found the remains of the brown duster Jayden and Mia saw. However, he couldn't stop the search for the coat just because they found this snap. The garment could be something other than the duster. His gut said this was the coat. But they would continue the searches.

~*~

After the kids finished their schoolwork and had lunch, Lil offered to take them on another horseback ride. Shandra knew she should get to work on the next pottery project, but she was feeling unsettled. She wasn't sure if it was having the twins around or the whole murder, but she didn't feel like being creative.

"I'm going to get groceries while you three are off riding," she said to Lil.

"You sure that's all you're gonna do?" The woman knew her too well.

"I might stop by and see Miranda. See how the pregnancy is going. With Alex so close to finding a cure for his disease, I'm sure he isn't home much." Shandra finished cleaning up the dishes thinking how she and Miranda had the cloud of losing their husbands over their heads. Shandra because of his job and Miranda because Alex had a hereditary condition that could kill him by age fifty-five if he didn't find the cure.

Lil and the kids left with Sheba in their wake. Shandra felt a little left out these days the way Sheba ignored her and followed the kids everywhere. She walked out to the barn to get the Jeep and stopped a moment, smiling.

The children were asking questions just as fast as Lil could answer. She was happy Lil was so comfortable around the kids.

"Mommy never took us anywhere except Aunt Andie's," Jayden said.

"Not to the store or the library?" Lil asked.

"She took us to that man's house," Mia said.

"What man?" Lil asked. It seemed she could be just as inquisitive as the children.

"She didn't take us to no man's house," Jayden emphasized.

"She did too!" Mia countered. "It was where she got the box under the rose bush."

Shandra stepped out where the three were getting horses ready to ride. "Thought I'd check and see if there was anything any of you wanted from town?"

Lil spun Mia to face Shandra. "You tell Shandra where the man lives. The one you say she got a box from."

Shandra glanced at Lil. How did she know that was important? "I can tell Ryan. It might be helpful."

"It was in Huckleberry. Mommy said Daddy called and wanted us to bring him lunch, but she stopped after giving Daddy a sandwich and chips she bought at a store." Mia's little face scrunched in disgust. "He coulda walked to a store and done the same thing."

"Where was the house?" Shandra coaxed.

"It wasn't really a house. It was the back of a building in town." Jayden said, finally jumping into the conversation.

"But a man opened the door when Mommy knocked. He smiled and Mommy walked in. We were sittin' in the car. That's what she told us to do." Mia nodded as if that was that.

"How long was she in the house?" Shandra asked.

"Long enough we were gettin' hot in the car. She took the keys, and we couldn't roll the windows down," Jayden said, grumpily. "She finally came out with the box. It was heavy, she wobbled carrying it, and yelled at me to open the trunk."

"Did she say anything about the box?"

"She told me it was my treasure chest to hide in my playhouse. Not to tell anyone or she'd take my doll away." Tears rimmed Mia's eyes.

"Don't worry, we won't take your doll away and your mom can't." Shandra pulled the child into a hug. She peered over the girl's head to her brother. "Do you remember anything about the building where your mom picked up the box?"

"It was down the street from where Daddy worked." Jayden drew the curry comb down Oliver's side. "She had something in there that would have made Daddy mad, didn't she?"

Shandra glanced at Lil. Her employee was a strong advocate for always telling the truth. Shandra was the same. "Yes. It was an illegal substance. Did she ever get anything out of the box or sell anything to other people?"

The two shook their heads.

"Ok. Thank you. What kind of donuts do you like?" Shandra asked.

"We only ever had the kind in a box with the white powder," Jayden said.

"Then I guess I'm going to have to buy one of every donut at the Daily Donut so you can sample and discover which will be your favorite."

Their small faces brightened and smiles spread, rounding their cheeks and showing off matching dimples.

"I'll be back before dinner," she said to Lil and headed to the Jeep.

She pulled the vehicle out of the barn and stopped to text Ryan. *I know where the box of drugs came from.*

He didn't reply. She put the Jeep in gear and headed to town.

~*~

Ryan sent Trapp to the state forensic lab in Coeur

d'Alene with the snaps and ashes from the fire pit. Speaks was to get lunch and meet him at the automotive shop by two.

"Did you find whatever you thought you'd find?" Teague asked, after settling his wife back in her bedroom.

"We didn't find exactly what we were looking for, but we did find items that will be tested at the lab." Ryan walked to the door.

Teague followed close on his heels. "I'm getting a lawyer. This is coming close to being harassment."

Ryan spun around as he opened the door. "I would think you'd want to discover who murdered your sister-in-law and her husband? It's odd your wife doesn't seem to care about her sister or her niece and nephew."

"We were never close with Jessica and her family. They lived differently than us."

The man's snobbery was starting to irritate Ryan. "There was nothing wrong with that family that a little more interaction between the sisters wouldn't have helped."

He walked briskly to his car and felt his phone vibrate. A text.

I know where the box of drugs came from.

Before starting up his vehicle, Ryan called Shandra.

"Hey, you must be busy," she answered.

"Yeah, just finished searching the Teague residence. How did you find out about the box?"

"I overheard a conversation between Lil and the kids. So, I stepped in and asked questions." The smugness in her voice made him smile.

"You're getting pretty good at getting information

out of those two."

"They want someone to listen to them. They haven't had that." Now her voice was filled with sadness.

"Yeah. So where did the box come from?"

"They said Jessica picked it up from a building down the street from where their Daddy worked. And the man who answered the door smiled at their Mommy." Her tone said she knew who it was.

He did too. "Don't go in. I'll be there in twenty minutes."

Chapter Twenty-three

Shandra had planned to invite Miranda down to Maxi's for an afternoon out. She could visit her friend and ask Maxine about the Webbs, but now she sat in front of Pop's Bar waiting for Ryan. If she went in before he arrived, he'd never tell her about any case again. While he said the owner, Steve, was sympathetic toward the family, she wondered how sympathetic if he gave Jessica a box of drugs worth half a million dollars to hide. She wondered now if he was more worried about the box than the family.

Ryan pulled up behind her Jeep. He stepped out and up to her driver's side door. "It would be best if you went on about whatever you planned to do in town."

She smiled. "You're funny. You know I'm not leaving. I'm going in there with you. I want to see this man who put a whole family in danger." She unlatched the door and gently pushed it open as Ryan stepped away.

"Let me do all the talking," Ryan said, grasping her hand and walking to the entrance of the bar.

The bar had opened while she'd sat waiting for Ryan. Two older men, who looked as if they frequented the bar every day, had entered.

They pushed open the door and stood a moment letting their eyes adjust to the darkness. The inside was all wood. Something she wouldn't have guessed from the metal exterior. It felt as if they were down in a mining shaft, minus the dirt and rock. The solid thick beams were set in arches every ten feet.

"It's a bit claustrophobic in here," she said, leaning toward Ryan for courage.

"We won't go any further." Ryan led her to the end of the bar closest to the door.

A man in his late twenties or early thirties came out of a room behind the bar. He smiled and walked the length of the bar. "Detective, I didn't expect to see you back in here. Didn't you catch up to Richard Webb?"

"I have some more questions about the Woodcock family. You seem to know more about them than anyone else." Ryan motioned to Shandra. "We'll have iced teas, please."

"Sure thing."

Shandra watched the man fix their drinks swiftly and efficiently. He was good at his job.

"Here you go." He placed the two glasses of iced tea in front of them. "What did you need to know?"

Ryan drank a third of his tea and said, "We were wondering why you gave Jessica a box of meth?"

His chin dropped, opening his mouth. He stuttered

for several seconds before his wits came back to him. "I didn't give her a box of meth. I talked her into getting cleaned up. Who said I did?"

Shandra worried that if Ryan said the kids, they'd be targets. Her fingers ached she squeezed the glass so hard, willing her husband not to mention the children.

"We found a hidden box at the Woodcock residence full of meth. We've learned she picked the box up from you." Ryan sipped his tea.

How he could be so cool, she didn't know, but it was one of the things she'd found fascinating about him from the first time they met.

"Was the box wood with a lid?" Steve asked.

"Yeah. About twenty by fifteen by eight inches."

The man's face lit up. "I don't know anything about drugs. I gave that box to Jessica filled with meat. Mitch had been in here for trivia night. He'd won and made the comment it would come in handy because he didn't get a deer tag and they were running low on meat. That tightwad Webb didn't pay Mitch near what he was worth. So I called Jessica and told her to come by here and I'd give them some meat. That box was full of frozen meat when she picked it up from me."

"Can anyone verify that?" Ryan asked.

"My sister. Angel wasn't happy I was helping out. She wanted the family to go down the tubes so she could get her hooks in Mitch."

"Is she here?" Ryan asked.

"She doesn't come in until five. Until then she waitresses at Maxi's."

Shandra grinned. "Have you had lunch?" she asked Ryan.

He glanced at his watch. "I'll have to make a call,

but I'll meet you there." He held out a hand to Steve. "Thanks for the information. It's nice to find someone who was looking out for the family."

The big man's eyes teared up. "If Jessica hadn't of married Mitch, I was going to ask her to marry me. I would have done anything for her. All she had to do was ask."

Shandra thought about that as she drove to Maxi's. Did Jessica realize she could have gotten out of the situation she was in if she had told Steve? Or was she one of those people who preferred to always be downtrodden?

There was plenty of parking in front of Maxi's. Shandra circled the block and parked at the Daily Donut. She'd called Mark, the owner of the bakery, while she was waiting for Ryan and asked him to box up one of every type he had left and she'd be by to pick them up. Depending on how long they were at Maxi's the bakery might be closed later.

She walked in and noticed two boxes setting on the counter behind the cash register.

"Shandra. I haven't seen Lil in a while, is that why you are purchasing one of everything?" Mark asked. For a baker, he was tall and thin. But he made the best donuts she'd ever eaten. And she wasn't the only one who thought so. The whole county raved about Mark's donuts and baked goods. The bakery had even been mentioned in several travel magazines since this was a town that made most of their income from tourists.

"Lil has been occupied. We have guests and that's who I'm buying the donuts for." She paid and he handed her the two boxes.

"If you don't have a lot of guests, you might not

want them to eat all of those in one sitting." He grinned.

"We're going to play a game." She smiled and headed out of the bakery. With the boxes stashed in the Jeep she walked back to Maxi's. Ryan pulled up to the curb as she crossed the street.

"Where did you park?" he asked.

"The bakery." She told him about taking the donuts to the twins.

"They are going to have a hard time deciding on a favorite." He put a hand on her back and they entered the trendy bar and restaurant run by their friend, Maxine.

Ryan spotted Angel as soon as they entered the establishment.

"Hey, you two. Long time no see." Maxine hurried over to them. She hugged them both.

Ryan always felt awkward when Maxine, with her double D breasts, hugged him. It was like there were two pillows between them. "Could you seat us in Angel's area?" he asked.

Maxine studied him a moment and bustled them over to a table by the front window. "What's been keeping you two away from town?"

Shandra smiled. "I've been working on pottery and Ryan's been busy."

The woman's usual brightness faded. "I heard about Jessica and Mitch. Have you learned anything? That is so sad. And the twins. They aren't going to that sister of hers, are they?"

Ryan studied Maxine. "What do you know about Andie?"

"She's always been a spoiled brat. First her mom and then Jessica worked themselves into the ground to make sure Andie had everything she wanted. I never understood why they didn't tell her 'no.'" She handed them menus. "I'll send Angel over." Maxine leaned close to Ryan. "She's not in trouble, is she?"

He shook his head. "No. I just have some questions for her."

Maxine's brilliant smile returned. "She'll be right over."

Shandra bumped Ryan's shoulder. "That's interesting about Jessica and her mom always doing what Andie wanted."

"Yeah. I wonder why?" Ryan made a mental note to see if the woman had an illness that brought on the migraines and if she'd had them longer than she'd told him.

Angel arrived beside their table. She started to prop the tray with the order pad against her hip and held it in front of her instead. "Detective, what can I get you?"

"My wife and I would like iced tea and I'll have a burger and fries." Ryan handed her the menus. "Can you tell me if your brother gave Jessica a box of meat?"

She stared at him.

"It was a wooden box with a lid. Did it have meat in it when your brother gave it to Jessica?" Ryan waited.

She tapped her pen on the order pad. "He not only gave her meat, he gave her milk when she came to the back door saying there wasn't any money left that month. He would have given her everything we had if she hadn't of died. The fool thought he could buy her love. She didn't want him, she wanted what he'd give her to keep those two brats alive. As long as she had them, she had Mitch." The woman whirled around and stomped to the kitchen.

"Wow! I could see her killing Jessica and watching her die in agony," Shandra said.

Ryan had to agree with his wife. She would kill Jessica to have Mitch, but she loved Mitch, so she didn't have a reason to kill him.

Chapter Twenty-four

Back home, Shandra pulled up to the back door of the house. It was evident Lil and the twins had returned from their ride. The horses were all in the corral, and Sheba ran out of the studio to greet her.

"Hey, girl. It's nice to see you do still remember me." She laughed as a large tongue licked her arm. "Where is everyone, I could use help carrying in the groceries."

"We're here!" Mia ran up to the Jeep. "What took you so long. We wanted a snack. Lil said we had to wait until you returned with the donuts."

"Everyone grab a bag. We'll have this unloaded in no time and then you can start sampling the donuts." Shandra handed the two boxes of donuts to Lil. She didn't trust Sheba to not knock them out of a smaller person's hands.

When the Jeep was unloaded and put away,

Shandra opened up the first box of donuts. "I'm going to cut the one you want to try in half. Then you both get a half and can decide which of them you like the best."

Mia pointed to a cream-filled, chocolate topped eclair. Shandra pulled it out and cut it in half.

Jayden, always practical, pointed at the glazed donut. Shandra took it out of the box and cut it in half.

"Hey what about me?" Lil asked, eyeing her favorite donut that was in the box.

"I forgot to ask Mark to give me extras of your favorite." Shandra laughed at the sight of the sixty-something woman pouting. "You can have the donut you like. The next time you go to town, you have to bring back ones for Jayden and Mia to try."

"Deal." Lil scooped the donut up so quick her hand was a blur.

Shandra put the groceries away while the twins ate the two halves and discussed what they liked and didn't like about each donut. She enjoyed listening to how they scientifically came up with their conclusions.

Mia nodded after eating the glazed donut. "I like mine the best."

Jayden nodded. "Mia picked the better donut."

"That means we know you would like an eclair over a glazed donut. After dinner you can try two more." Shandra pulled out items to make salad. "Let's get started on dinner."

The two washed their hands and knelt on the stools to help.

Lil had disappeared after scooping up the donut.

While driving home, Shandra had bounced around the information she'd learned today. She really didn't have anything to ask the children except how had the meth got in the box that had been used to haul meat home? And she couldn't come out and ask it that way.

While they peeled carrots and chopped celery, Shandra asked, "Did anyone come to your house regularly?"

"Mr. Parson would come check on us once a week. Sometimes we'd see him and the dogs a couple times in a week," Jayden said. "He liked to let them run through the forest between our houses."

"Did he ever visit with your mom?" Shandra ripped lettuce for the salad.

"He'd come in for a cup of coffee when Daddy wasn't home." Mia wrinkled her nose. "He always smelled. Daddy said it was because he didn't have a wife anymore and didn't care."

"Did anyone else ever visit?"

They both shook their heads.

They all tossed their ingredients into the salad and Shandra told them they could go off to play until Ryan came home. When the twins ran out of the house with Sheba, she picked up her phone and texted Ryan. *The kids say the only person who visited often was the neighbor, Mr. Parson.*

~*~

"What do you mean you have a warrant to search my shop?" Mr. Webb bellowed. It was this reaction that Ryan had prepared for. He not only had Deputy Speaks, but also Huckleberry Chief of Police Sandberg and Officer Blane to help pacify the owner and to get the search done quicker. From here they'd go to the Webb residence.

Chief Sandberg took Webb to the side.

"You can go home for the day," Ryan told the

employee, Ray.

He nodded and walked out the door.

Speaks, Blaine, and Ryan each took a third of the shop and searched through everything looking for anything that resembled a brown coat or remnants of the monkshood plant.

"What are you looking for?" Webb asked.

"Evidence." Ryan had finished his section of the shop. Nothing. He had a feeling the snaps and ashes they found at the Teague's was the coat they were looking for, but he wanted to make sure his other suspects weren't the killers before he turned all his attention to the not-so grieving sister.

They finished the search after two hours. It was past five and he still had to search the house. Ryan pulled out his phone to let Shandra know he would be late, again, and saw a text from her.

When the officers had all regrouped in front of the Webb residence, he pulled Chief Sandberg to the side. "Would you go dig up everything you can find on Jerry Parson? He was neighbors to the Woodcocks. Speaks, Blaine, and I can handle it from here."

The chief nodded and headed back to his car.

Ryan knocked on the door.

Mrs. Webb opened the door and stepped back. "I've been expecting you."

"Did your husband call you?" Ryan hadn't seen the man on the phone.

"No, Ray called me."

"You'll have to step outside while we do the search." Ryan handed her the warrant to search the house.

She took the paper, didn't read it, and walked over

to the porch swing and sat. "I had no reason to want
either Jessica or Mitch dead. The bedroom at the end of
the hall on the right is my husband's. Whatever you're
looking for would most likely be in there."

Ryan shared a glance with Speaks. They headed
straight back to the room at the end of the hall on the
right. Blaine stayed on the porch with Mrs. Webb.

~*~

Shandra once again, tucked the kids in and
promised Ryan would come in to say good-night when
he came home. Getting to try two more donuts had
lessened their disappointment that Ryan would be home
late again. It was something she'd become used to as
the wife of a county detective. When he had a murder
investigation or was called out to help with other
disputes, she knew he'd be home when he was finished.
It would be hard for a child to understand. Maybe they
were only cut out to be foster parents. Help children get
on their feet before going to a permanent home.

She pulled her computer onto her lap and searched
the Huckleberry and Warner newspaper archives for
Jerry Parson. Back fifteen years, he was a teacher at
Warner High. He also coached football. He would have
been Mitch's coach. The one that helped him get a
college scholarship to play football. Funny. If he was
Mitch's coach, why did he visit the Woodcock's when
Mitch was as work?

Lights flashed through the front window. Ryan was
home. She closed the computer and walked in the
kitchen to get Ryan's dinner out of the oven.

The back door opened and closed. His footsteps
started down the hall and disappeared.

Shandra smiled. He'd gone in to tell the kids

goodnight.

The footsteps resumed and he walked into the kitchen. "Sorry I'm so late." He kissed her and walked around to sit at the counter.

"I know you're busy." She placed the plate that had been warming in front of him and headed to the refrigerator to get the salad.

"Did the kids eat all the donuts?"

She spun around. "No. I should have bought two of everything. Lil already snatched one."

Ryan laughed. "I don't have to have one. But it sounds like a good dessert when I finish this."

Shandra set iced tea in front of him and placed a donut box on the counter. "At the rate I'm doling out the donuts, getting one of everything wasn't a good idea. By the time they get to the last ones they'll be hard and stale." She picked out the cinnamon twist for her dessert.

"Did you find anything?" She bit into the twist, loving the bright cinnamon heat.

"Possibly the coat both children saw. But it was burned up." Ryan scooped a bite into his mouth.

"Where?" Shandra was pulling for the aunt to not be involved.

"The Teague's. Bradley took a swing at Trapp when I sent him around back. We found the ashes still smoldering in a firepit and metal snaps."

"I was hoping they didn't have anything to do with it for the twin's sake."

He sighed and picked up his drink. "Yeah, me, too." He drank half the glass. "I asked forensics to make the ashes and snaps a priority. I'd like to get this cleared up."

"I was looking up Jerry Parson. He was a teacher and a football coach when Mitch and Andie were in school. I was wondering why he only came around to see the Woodcocks when Mitch was at work. You'd think he would have gone around when his star football player was around." She finished off her donut.

Ryan grabbed an apple fritter from the box. "I had Chief Sandberg dig up what he could find on him. It should be in an email." He waved his hand, holding his iced tea, toward the great room. "Shall we go see what he had to say?"

Shandra jumped up, putting the dishes in the sink and the salad back in the refrigerator, before joining Ryan at the dining room table. He had his laptop out and was munching on the fritter.

"What did he find?" Shandra pulled a chair over next to him.

"It appears Mr. Parson was caught selling meth ten years ago. Right before his wife passed away. Looks like she had cancer and the hospital bills piled up. He said he did it to pay his bills." Ryan glanced at her. "He was sentenced to seven years. He's been out three and so far clean, but he sounds like a good place to look for the meth."

Shandra walked over to the couch, grabbed her computer, and looked up Warner High School teachers fifteen years earlier. "He's making the meth," she said, pointing to a photo of him. Under the photo it said: Mr. Parson, Science Teacher.

"No wonder he prowls around in the woods. He probably has something set up at the back of his property." Ryan ran a hand over his face. "But why was he having Jessica keep it for him?"

"A question to ask someone on the drug task force maybe?" Shandra suggested. She closed both their computers. "Tomorrow."

Chapter Twenty-five

Jayden and Mia sat at the counter when Ryan walked in to the kitchen the next morning.

"Did you learn anything yesterday?" Jayden asked.

Ryan knew he meant about his parents' murders but he couldn't resist teasing. "I learned that Shandra used getting you two donuts to go to town and make me eat lunch."

The twins started laughing. Shandra threw the hand towel at him.

Jayden's laugh slowed and he said, "No, I mean about what happened to Mommy and Daddy."

"I'm working on it. That's the problem with bad people who do bad things. They work harder at covering up what they did than the planning. We'll get it figured out soon." He put a hand on their shoulders.

"You'll tell us who did it?" Jayden stared up into his eyes. The truth was important to the boy.

"I will tell you the truth." Ryan squeezed his shoulder and sat down.

"Good. Mommy and Daddy always told lies." The boy frowned.

"They thought we were too little to know, but we did," Mia confirmed.

"What were some of the lies?" Ryan asked.

"I asked Daddy why Mommy didn't like us and he said she did, she just had a different way of showing it." Mia glanced at both he and Shandra. "She never did nice things for us like you and Daddy."

"I asked Daddy why we always go to the cabin on the weekends. He said to give Mommy time to herself." Jayden shook his head. "He didn't like being around Mommy."

"When I asked Mommy why she was always tired and didn't eat, she said it was so she could stay pretty for Daddy." Mia pushed her plate away from her. "We saw her put needles in her arm. She said she wore long-sleeved shirts because she was cold."

Ryan decided to stop this. It was evident the adults in their lives had never told them a single thing that was the truth. "We," he pointed to Shandra and himself, "will always tell you the truth. Even if it might make you sad."

"Yes," Shandra said, putting an arm around Mia, hugging her and then patting Jayden. "I was lied to as a child as well. I understand the need to be told the truth."

They both stared at her. "You were?"

"I was. It's a story I can tell you while I work in the studio and you do your schoolwork."

"Lil showed us how to glaze coasters yesterday while you were gone," Mia said.

"I bet she did. One less thing for her to do," Ryan said.

Mia glared at him. "That's not nice. Lil works hard and is nice."

Ryan put his hands up in surrender. "You're right. I need to eat and get to work. I'm hoping to have some news for you tonight when I get home."

"By dinner?" Mia asked.

"I can't make any promises on that, but I will try." Ryan ate his breakfast while Shandra and the children chatted about how they planned to spend their day. When he finished, he stood, gave each of the children a pat on the back, dropped a kiss on Shandra's cheek, and entered the great room to get his computer and bag.

Straightening, he found Jayden standing halfway in the room.

Ryan walked over to the boy. "What's wrong?"

"I have a feeling what you are going to tell us about our parents isn't going to be good."

"Why do you say that?" Ryan put a hand on his small shoulder.

"They fought a lot. We'd go outside or to our room but we could hear them. Daddy had a girlfriend and Mommy had a drug dealer. They argued about everything. Even us. Mommy wanted to give us back." The boy studied Ryan's face. "What did she mean by that?"

He wasn't ready to tell them what he'd dug up yet. "Now isn't the time to discuss it. But I promise, when I've put the person who killed your parents in jail, I will tell you everything I know." He put out a hand to shake. "Deal?"

Jayden glanced from Ryan's hand to his eyes and

put his small hand against Ryan's palm. They shook. "Deal."

"Have fun today. Forget about the bad times. There will only be people who love you and care for what's best for you ahead."

The boy threw his arms around Ryan's waist.

He hugged the boy with one arm.

"Jayden?" Shandra stepped into the great room. Her heart filled with joy at the sight of Ryan and Jayden hugging. She could tell something was on the boy's mind when he'd left the kitchen.

Ryan glanced up at her. The emotions in his eyes, struck her. She had a feeling the twins wouldn't be leaving here any time soon.

"I have to go." Ryan released the boy and Jayden stepped back.

"See you tonight," Shandra said, walking up to Jayden and putting an arm around his shoulders.

"I'll be here as soon as I can." Ryan walked out the door.

"Well, are you ready to help Lil feed the horses?" Shandra asked.

"Yeah. Where's Mia?" Jayden pulled away from her and headed to the hall.

"She's already out there."

"Without me?" He took off running down the hall. She heard him hit the back door and slam it shut.

Shandra stood in the great room, wondering what the two men in her life had been talking about. She glanced at her laptop and hoped Ryan was able to pull everything together soon. The twins needed to be able to move on.

~*~

Ryan headed for the Sheriff's Office. He'd pretty much completed all the police footwork he could on this case. It was now a matter of waiting for forensics and gathering information.

At the Sheriff's Office, Cathleen stopped him. "How's the fostering going?"

"Good. Those two deserve people in their life who care about them. Not just treat them as a mistake." Ryan had thought about what the children had said about their parents and wondered how many other damaging things they'd overheard.

"Wow. You're pretty emotional about those two." She stared into his eyes. "Little brother what are you and Shandra thinking?"

"Nothing I'm going to tell you. Yet." He winked at his sister and strode down the hall to his office.

Several folders sat on his desk. The light on his desk phone was blinking. He listened to the message.

"Detective Greer, this is Sheila Rickman, I have some more information about your victims. Give me a call when you get this."

He pulled out his cell phone and hit the number he had saved for the forensic pathologist.

"Hello?"

"Sheila, this is Detective Greer. What did you find on my victims?"

"The female had never had children. Your report said you were looking for twins."

"I've discovered she wasn't the mother of the two children." Ryan had hoped she would have something more than what he already knew.

"Her internal organs were about to give out." The woman sounded preoccupied. As if she were doing something else as she talked.

"Are you saying you think it was suicide now?"

"No. It was the monkshood that killed her. The slices were superficial, only made to get the poison in her system faster. But some bruising showed up that makes me think she may have been restrained while the cutting was done."

"Do you think there were two people? One holding her down and one cutting?" Ryan wondered if this had been done by one of the couples he was investigating.

"No. One person. The bruising indicates marks similar to cording."

This fit his theory that whoever did it stayed around to clean up afterward, to make the scene look like suicide. This wasn't a spur of the moment thing. It was thought out down to the cording and cleaning up the vomit.

Papers being flipped came through the phone. "Now your male victim. He was healthy, strong, and virile. My guess is he'd had a vasectomy about ten years ago, give or take a few years."

Ryan's head spun. "The kids that everyone says are his were conceived eight years ago, or there about."

"He could have got snipped right after the woman became pregnant. But you might want to do a DNA swab on the kids to make sure this is their biological father. You know, so whoever adopts them can know the family medical history."

"Was that the big news you called me about?" It really didn't have anything to do with the murder, that he could think of. After all, it had happened a long time ago, but if he was shooting blanks, he didn't have to worry about anyone he slept with getting pregnant.

Ryan was beginning to think Mitch might have been more of a player than he'd first thought.

"No. We know the shotgun you bagged is where the fatal blast came from. The tech guys found bird shot in the shells you bagged at the cabin. They determined from the BBs I pulled out of the body that it was double-aught that killed him."

"Someone slipped a more powerful shot cartridge into the gun before shooting him? That doesn't make sense. When would they have done that? While they were talking to him, and he just sat there grinning, not expecting whoever it was to shoot him?" He was rambling but his mind was spinning. Someone wanted to make sure he was dead. Someone who knew enough to slip buckshot in the gun.

"That's all I have for you. Thought you might be able to do something with that." The pathologist ended the call.

Ryan rubbed a hand over his face. He wondered if anyone who'd helped him search the Teague and Webb residences yesterday saw a box of double-aught cartridges.

Chapter Twenty-six

Lil walked into the studio right after Shandra had
the twins seated in the area where she worked on
drawing ideas for potential vases she wanted to make.
They had their workbooks and text books stacked on
the small table between the two chairs. For a long time
there had only been one chair, but once Ryan moved in,
she'd added the other chair so he would feel welcome
to visit her in the studio.

"What you making these two varmints do?" Lil
asked, walking over to where the twins sat.

"Their schoolwork. Then they can glaze coasters
when they finish, if they want." Shandra smiled at the
two bobbing heads.

"I was hoping someone could go for a horseback
ride with me." Lil grabbed the old metal folding chair
she sat on when she stirred the glaze and set it between
the two kids. "Guess I'll have to help speed up the

schoolwork.”

“Lil, don’t you give them any answers,” Shandra said, as she wedged the clay she would use on her next project—a set of twin vases.

“She doesn’t give us the answers,” Jayden said as they both pulled out their reading books and began reading. They took turns, one reading a paragraph and the other sibling reading the next paragraph with Lil correcting wrong pronunciations or words.

Shandra hummed and continued preparing the clay.

~*~

Ryan talked to Trapp, Speaks, and Blaine. Blaine said he’d noticed shotgun shells at the Webb residence in the closet with the gun safe. But he didn’t pay attention to what kind they were. He hadn’t known shotgun shells were relevant to the case. He hadn’t been privy to the reports on the case because it was being handled by the county. Ryan hung up from talking to the city cop and smiled. That young cop’s nose was out of joint over not knowing everything that was going on. Trapp said he hadn’t noticed any guns or ammunition at the Teague residence.

If the shotgun shells were at the Webb residence, Ryan was positive Mrs. Webb would let him in to look at them. But he couldn’t find a connection other than Mitch working for Webb and bedding his wife. There wasn’t any connection to Jessica. He didn’t see Mr. Webb killing Mitch and Jessica. And given the evidence, the same person had killed both.

His money was still on Andie Teague.

He walked into dispatch and asked to use the radio. Cathleen backed up and opened her arms wide.

“Patrol, this is Detective Greer. While you’re out

riding around, stop in at every store in the county that sells shotgun shells and see if the photos I'm sending you bought any double-aught cartridges."

"Copy."

"Copy."

"Copy."

He turned to Cathleen. "Who is out on patrol?"

She told him the three, and he sent photos of the Teagues and Webbs to the deputies. "I'm headed to Huckleberry to see if the shells Blaine saw at the Webb residence are double-aught."

"I'll let the sheriff know."

Ryan walked out to his vehicle and called Shandra.

The phone rang several times before a young voice said, "Hello, this is Shandra, the potter's, answering service." Mia started giggling.

Ryan laughed. "I see. Is Shandra the potter busy? I'd like to speak to her."

"She's washing her hands."

"Did you like my answering service?" Shandra asked with laughter in her voice.

"It was unique and adorable."

"Mia, he said you were adorable." Her voice was muted. Then louder, clearer. "What's up?"

"I'm headed back to Huckleberry to check on something. Is there a chance you could bring the kids to town? I want to do a DNA swab." Her intake of breath told him she had questions.

"That shouldn't be a problem." She groaned. "Except Lil wanted to take them riding when they finished their schoolwork."

"Bring them in for lunch and take them straight home afterward. She can take them for a ride when you get back. Tell them I want to have lunch with them in case I can't make dinner."

"Ok. Ruthie's at noon?" she asked.

"It's a date." Ryan started his vehicle and headed to Huckleberry. He had enough time to go by the Webb's before meeting Shandra and the kids.

~*~

The twins insisted Sheba needed an outing to town as well. The three sat in the back seat, Sheba in the middle, her tongue hanging out and looking as happy as Shandra had ever seen the goofy mutt. The dog loved riding in the Jeep, but she loved the two children sitting on either side of her more.

"When we get shown our booth at Ruthie's, you both need to go into the restroom and wash your hands," Shandra said as she parked in front of the diner.

The twins stared at the building.

"We're going in there to eat?" Jayden asked, not unbuckling.

"Yes. Ruthie, the woman who owns the diner, is one of my best friends. You'll like her. And her little boy, Donnie." She opened the door and slid out.

The two remained inside the car.

"Come on! Don't you want a burger and a shake?"
They both nodded.

"We've never eaten anywhere but at home and school. And your house," Mia said.

"Then think of this as a new adventure." Shandra led the two into the building.

Ruthie walked up to them. It was early for the lunch crowd, giving them their choice of the booths. "Shandra, who have you brought to my diner?"

Shandra put a hand on the twins' shoulders.

191

"Ruthie, this is Jayden and Mia. They are staying with us for a while."

Her friend shook hands with each child. "Welcome to my diner. You know, Shandra comes here all the time. I think she likes my caramel milkshakes better than she likes me."

The two children giggled.

"I adore you, but your milkshakes I love." Shandra hugged her friend. "Ryan is joining us."

"Then let's put you all in the booth over here." Ruthie indicated the booth Shandra liked, where she could see everyone in the diner and watch who entered.

Just as Jayden started to slid in, he popped back out. "Wash our hands," he said to his sister.

"Over there," Ruthie said, pointing to the short hall to the restrooms.

The kids disappeared and Ruthie slid into the booth. "Are those the two that lost their parents?"

"Yes. Every time they tell something else about their life with their parents it breaks my heart." Shandra glanced toward the restrooms. "They have never been in a restaurant before."

"Well, their dad frequented the diner. You would have thought he could have brought his children and not flirted with a woman." Ruthie's golden-brown complexion reddened with anger.

"What woman? Mrs. Webb?" Shandra had thought those two kept their liaisons secret.

"No. Mrs. Webb doesn't like her husband but she wouldn't sleep around. Angel. She waitresses at Maxi's and works at her family's bar on second street. Pop's, I think is what it's called."

Jayden returned and stood beside the booth.

Ruthie slid out and he slid in.

"Where's Mia?" he asked.

"Making her hands nice and clean, I guess," Shandra said, also wondering what was keeping the girl.

"You watch for Ryan. I'll go see what's keeping her." Shandra walked to the restroom and entered.

The child stood in front of the hand dryer, watching her hair blow, in the mirror. She jumped when Shandra appeared.

"I'm coming," she said and hurried to the door.

"It's okay. You're not in trouble. I just wondered what was keeping you." Shandra followed the girl out into the restaurant.

Ryan sat in the booth beside Jayden, talking.

She and Mia slid in across from them. Shandra had hoped to tell him about Angel, if they sat side by side.

"Ready to order?" Ruthie asked, smiling at them as if they were all about to embark on an amusement park ride.

"We need some time to look at the menu," Shandra said, knowing the children hadn't a clue what to order.

"I'll get your drinks then." Ruthie glanced at Mia. "What would you like?"

"Water." The child ducked her head.

Shandra turned the menu over. "They have soda pop, milk shakes, milk, juice. Wouldn't you like to have one of those rather than water that you can drink any time?"

"I've never had a milkshake. Do you take milk and shake it?" Mia peered at Ruthie.

"Darling, we put vanilla ice cream in a big metal glass, add milk, and whatever flavor you want." She pointed to the list of flavors on the menu.

Shandra read off the flavors. "What do you think? Would you like one of those?"

Mia stared across the table at her brother. "Do you want to try the strawberry one?"

He nodded.

"That will be one strawberry milkshake and two cups." Ruthie smiled. "That's a good choice. Strawberry is my favorite." She turned her gaze on Ryan. "And you?"

"Iced tea, please."

Shandra grinned at her friend. "You know what I want."

"And a caramel milkshake. I'll get those made and when I bring them out you can tell me what you want to eat." Ruthie hurried behind the counter.

"Where's Donnie?" Ryan asked.

"I don't know. I should have asked." Shandra glanced to the corner where a playpen sat. That was where Donnie took naps or played when he wasn't in the pack on his mother's back.

"What did you two do this morning?" Ryan asked.

The kids filled him in on their schoolwork while Shandra figured out how to mention Angel to Ryan.

Ruthie returned with the drinks.

The twins sipped and grinned from ear to ear.

"This is better than I expected," Mia said.

"Yeah!" Jayden latched onto the straw and drew in another swallow.

Ryan order cheeseburgers and fries as Maxwell entered the diner carrying Donnie.

"Looks like Maxwell got some Donnie time today," Shandra said.

"Yes. He's been dying to take Donnie to the park even though he's only able to stand and waddle a short distance." Ruthie's gaze was on her two men.

Maxwell walked over after depositing the sleeping Donnie in the playpen. "Hey, what's the deal not inviting me to this party?"

Jayden tipped his head back and stared up at the six-foot-six man. "You're even bigger than my daddy. He played football. Did you play football?"

Maxwell showed off his full set of large white teeth as he smiled and then said, "Yeah, I played in high school. Didn't want to deal with trying to play and keep up my grades in college. Who's your daddy?"

"Mitch Woodcock," Jayden said, his chin tipping down.

Maxwell's eyes widened, but he caught his surprise and put a hand on the boy's shoulder. "He was a heck of a good ball player."

"Come on, Maxwell. Come tell me all about Donnie playing at the park." Ruthie pulled her husband away from the now somber group at the table.

"Why did Jayden saying Daddy's name surprise that man?" Mia asked.

Shandra peered across the table at Ryan.

He cleared his throat. "Maxwell, Mr. Treat, and his father own the mortuary in town. He came out and picked up your daddy to get him ready for his funeral."

"What's a funeral?" Mia asked.

Shandra took over. "It's where family and friends get to say good-bye to a loved one who has died."

"When is Daddy and Mommy's funeral?" Mia asked.

"That is up to the next of kin. Your aunt Andie and

grandparents." Shandra wondered that they hadn't heard anything from the grandparents. They'd had the children living with them for several days now.

"Aren't we next of kin? We're their kids," Jayden said.

"Yes, but it's something an adult has to arrange." Shandra glanced at Ryan. He gave her a nod as if saying she was doing okay.

"Oh." Jayden was quiet for the rest of lunch.

Shandra was thinking about sending the kids out to the Jeep with some fries for Sheba to get a minute to speak with Ryan when Ruthie came over and ask if they'd like to see how the milkshakes were made.

Both children said they would and followed Ruthie over to the counter. She had them climb up on stools and watch as she talked them through how to make a milkshake.

Shandra took this moment to lean across the table. "I learned that Angel, the waitress at Maxi's, met Mitch in here a few times."

"I already knew she had a thing for Mitch." Ryan grinned. "Where did you hear that information?" He plucked the straws out of the twins' empty drink cups, folded them in half, and rolled them up in separate napkins before putting them in his jacket pocket.

"From Ruthie while the kids were washing their hands in the restroom." Shandra leaned back as the kids came skipping back to the table.

"I have to get back to work." Ryan stood and peered down at the twins. "I'll try to be home before you go to bed tonight, but I can't make promises when I'm working on a case."

"We understand. What you do is important to

people like us," Jayden said.

Mia hugged him around the waist.

Shandra's grin hurt from the corners of her lips turning up so much. The look on Ryan's face was one she would never forget. Pride, embarrassment, and acceptance.

"I have to go. See you later." He patted the kids on the head and kissed Shandra before striding out the door.

Ruthie walked by and quietly said, "That man is hooked."

Shandra laughed. "Yes, he is."

"Is what?" Mia asked. Her little ears heard a lot.

"A good man. Come on. If I don't get you back in time for you to ride horses with Lil, I'll never hear the end of it." Shandra herded the two out to the Jeep where Sheba was very happy to see them when they each presented her with a fistful of fries.

Chapter Twenty-seven

The trip to the Webb residence before lunch had been a bust. The shells Blaine had seen weren't the type that killed Mitch.

Sitting in his vehicle, deciding which direction to go next, his phone buzzed. State forensics.

"Greer."

"This is Dennis at the State Forensic Lab. I think I've determined the jacket that was burned up yesterday was an oilskin duster. The snaps were verified by the company that makes the duster. I couldn't tell you the color by the ashes but they do come in brown. The snaps are made in two pieces and pressed together. In the seam of the press, I found dried blood. It was a small amount that had been baked, not sure I can match it to either victim."

Ryan stared forward as he listened to the technician go on about how certain elements in the blood were compromised by the heat. Even though his gut told him that Andie was lying, he hadn't wanted her to be the murderer for the kids' sake.

Dennis finished. "I'll have all of this written up and emailed to you in an hour."

"Thanks. I'm sending you two drink straws to match the DNA on the victims."

"Will deal with it when it arrives."

The line went dead. Ryan dialed Sheriff Oldham. "Send a car to request the Teagues come in for questioning. I'll be there by the time a car brings them in."

~*~

When they returned home, Lil had all the horses saddled and ready to ride. Shandra thanked the woman as the twins argued over who would sit in the saddle and rein Oliver.

"How about Mia sit in front on the way out and Jayden you can have the reins on the way back. You're stronger and can keep Oliver from getting in too big of a hurry to get home."

The boy grinned and stuck his tongue out at his sister. But Mia was happy to be first and hadn't heard what Shandra had said.

Lil took the lead on Duke, with Oliver behind her, and Shandra riding Apple in the back. It was a beautiful afternoon for early summer. The wildflowers had started to bloom and the warmth had the pine trees emitting their glorious nose tingling scent.

Sheba trotted ahead of Lil to start with then fell back to walk alongside Oliver. Shandra shook her head and smiled at how courageous the dog had become now that there were two people smaller than her who needed protecting.

Lil stopped at the small meadow about two miles above the house. A trickle of snowmelt divided the meadow in two. "Shall we rest our backsides here?" she asked.

"Sounds good to me." Shandra dismounted and headed to help the children down.

Jayden slid around his sister, missed the stirrup and fell to the ground, dragging his sister down on top of him.

Mia started wailing as soon as she hit the ground.

Shandra's heart flew to her throat. She knelt by the two children. Mia was screaming her arm hurt, but Jayden wasn't moving.

"Don't move him," Lil said, sitting Mia up. "Where do you hurt?" She directed the question to the girl. When the child just kept wailing, Lil grabbed her chin and put her face close to Mia's. "Where does your arm hurt? We can't help you if you don't tell us."

Mia quit screaming and pointed with her right hand to her left shoulder.

"Collar bone," Lil said, untying the bandana wrapped around her neck. "Make a sling and put her left arm in it."

Shandra was in as much shock as the two children, but more so because of Lil's matter-of-fact treatment of the child. She measured the length at which to tie the bandana, slid it over Mia's head and urged her to slide her arm in.

"It hurts," the child cried.

"It will only hurt putting it in. Once you have the scarf to hold it up, it won't hurt no more," Lil said, carefully feeling Jayden's limbs.

Mia finally slid her arm in with a cry and then just sniffed.

"I'm going to take Oliver's headstall off and let him follow us back down. You take Mia on your horse with you. I'll take Jayden." Lil took off Oliver's headstall, tying it on the saddle horn.

Then she walked over and mounted her horse. "Lift him up to me."

Shandra slid her arms under the boy's shoulders and knees and lifted him up to Lil. She hadn't realized how light he was until this moment. The older woman cradled Jayden in her arms as if she did this every day.

"You help Mia into the saddle and you mount up behind her." Lil headed down the trail.

Shandra helped Mia up with only one cry of discomfort from the child. Then mounted behind the saddle and followed Lil. Sheba trotted along beside Lil, whimpering. At least the klutzy dog had stayed back while they dealt with the children.

~*~

Ryan reached the Sheriff's Office as the Teagues were being escorted into the station. The husband looked furious. Andie looked as pale as he'd seen her. He wondered if she needed to see a doctor rather than take herbs for her headache.

"What is the meaning of this?" Bradley Teague demanded.

"I have some questions for you and your wife. Ones that I thought would best be answered here." Ryan motioned for the husband to go ahead of him down the hall. "Mrs. Teague, you can wait in the other room. It will be quieter and I can have the lights left off."

"Thank you," the woman murmured.

Cathleen escorted Andie into the interview room next to the break room.

"Do I need to call a lawyer?" Teague asked when Ryan entered the room.

"That's up to you. I have some questions that are bugging me."

"Questions you couldn't ask at our house? You know making us come here, to the police station, makes us look guilty." Teague hadn't sat down. He paced back and forth.

"Have a seat. Are you guilty?" Ryan sat down, dropping the file of the two murders on the table.

"Not of killing anyone." Teague pointed to the two folders with Mitch and Jessica's names on them.

"What are you guilty of?" Ryan pulled out a photo of one of the snaps they'd dug out of the firepit.

Teague stopped pacing, sat down, and stared at the photo. He dropped it to the table. "That doesn't prove she did it."

"That your wife killed Mitch and her sister?"

The man glared at him. "She doesn't have it in her to kill anyone. Have you seen her lately? Those headaches take everything out of her."

"Then why did you burn the coat, evidence in two homicides, if you didn't think she did it?" Ryan left the photo sitting on the table. "They found blood on a snap."

"There was blood on the coat. That's why I burned it." Teague ran a hand through his hair. "I love Andie. She wouldn't kill anyone, I know it."

"But..." Ryan waited.

"This headache. She's had it ever since they were

killed. Stress brings on her headaches. I wouldn't have even thought it of her if the headache had gone away after she slept. But you saw her when she came in here. She's weak, can't sleep, can't eat. She's a wreck."

"So, you started digging around the house since she was hiding out in the bedroom." Ryan urged the man to talk.

"Yeah. I found that coat tucked under a bush by the herb garden. I didn't know if it was even Andie's. But when I saw the blood and put that and the headache together. I wanted to get rid of it and tell her everything would be okay. But you showed up with the warrant."

Ryan pulled out a photo of the monkshood plant he'd photographed in the Teague herb garden. "Why do you grow a poisonous plant in your herb garden?"

"We use that to kill rodents. I dip cheese in the liquid and leave it out. We haven't had a rodent problem since I discovered this." The man looked pleased with himself.

"That's what killed Jessica. She was poisoned with monkshood."

Teague's face contorted and he shook his head. "You think because we grow this that we…?"

"Are you saying you and Andie killed her sister and brother-in-law?" Ryan stared at the man. He wasn't hiding any emotions. His eyes were vibrating as his mind was spinning behind his eyeballs.

"No. We didn't kill either of them. I heard Mitch was shot. We don't even own a gun. And why would we want to kill him? We don't want to take on the kids." He made a face as if the children were no better than the rodents he poisoned.

"But you burned a coat that was evidence in a

murder investigation because you thought your wife had killed someone." Ryan studied him.

"No. I-I found it and burned it because it was no longer fit to wear."

"Why didn't you ask your wife if it was her coat?" That was bugging Ryan. If he found something compromising, he'd ask Shandra if it was hers.

"She's been keeping secrets. I know. I can tell. I don't want to pry and have her leave me." The man's usual stony demeanor softened. "I love that woman, faults and all."

Ryan stood up. "Maybe you should tell her that."

Teague stared at him. "What do you know? Was she secretly seeing Mitch?"

"I don't know, but she does have secrets you might want to ask her about." He scooped up the files. "After I talk to her."

Ryan walked down the hall and entered the darkened interview room.

Andie glanced up. She held a paper cup of water in her hands on the table in front of her.

"You know, if you unburdened your worries to your husband, I bet that headache would go away." Ryan sat down.

She sipped the water. "Or it could get worse."

"I just talked to your husband."

Her head whipped up and she winced. "You didn't tell him about Mitch and the kids, did you?"

"No, that's yours to tell. But from the way he's been trying to protect you, I'd say he won't toss you out." Ryan opened the file and pulled out a photo of a duster like the one they believed was worn by the murderer. "Do you own a coat like this?"

Andie stared at the photo. "It's hard to see in the dim light."

"I can turn the lights on."

"Ok. I want to see what it looks like." Andie picked up the paper but shaded her eyes with the other hand.

Ryan stood and flipped on the light.

The woman winced at the brightness but studied the photo. "I've never owned a coat like this. Isn't it what cowboys wear?"

"Any idea how one became shoved under the hedge by your herb garden?"

She stared at the photo.

"One with blood on it?"

Her gaze came up to his. "Blood? Whose?"

"Mitch and your sister."

She dropped the photo. "You think-I-we had our arguments. And when Mitch lost his job, he came to me asking for child support. I couldn't tell Bradley. But I didn't kill him. And I didn't kill my sister." She put her hand over her eyes. "You want to know why I can't get rid of this freakin' headache? It's guilt. But not because I killed them. It's because all I could think of when I heard they were dead. was my past will be buried with them. My guilt is over being happy they are gone."

Chapter Twenty-eight

Ryan's phone buzzed as he stepped out of the interview room. Shandra had left a voice message. He hit the button to listen.

"Ryan, we're headed to the clinic. The kids fell off Oliver."

He tossed the folders on his desk and jogged to the front of the building.

"What's wrong?" Cathleen asked from the dispatch office.

"Kids are hurt. I'll be at the Huckleberry Clinic." He hopped into his vehicle, turned on his lights, and drove as fast as he could to Huckleberry.

~*~

Shandra stood between the two beds in the emergency side of the clinic. Alex, Dr. Porter, was checking Jayden's vital signs while Chandler, Maxwell's brother, and nurse in the emergency side of the clinic, put a proper sling on Mia.

"You say they fell off a horse?" Alex asked.

"Yes. We'd stopped and before I got off and over to help them, Jayden tried getting off himself and ended up pulling Mia down on top of him." Shandra smiled at Mia, and returned her attention to the boy.

She could hear Lil's boots clomping back and forth in the waiting area. Alex would only allow one of them in the examination area.

"Did you see if he hit his head on a rock or log?" Alex continued probing and looking the boy over.

"No. It looked like just dirt and meadow grass under him. Is he going to be alright?" Shandra's stomach had been clenching and unclenching all the way into town.

Alex looked over at Mia. "Did your head hit your brother's?"

"My head doesn't hurt. Only my arm." She stuck her bottom lip out in a pout, and Chandler handed her a sucker with a sympathetic smile.

"From what you tell me, he should come to soon. I'll keep him here until he does." Alex nodded to Chandler. "Keep an eye on him. Check his vitals every fifteen minutes and call over to the clinic when he comes around."

"Will do." Chandler placed a stool in front of Mia's bed. "You can get down if you want."

She shook her head. "I'm not leaving Jayden. He's all I got." A tear trickled down her cheek.

Shandra walked over and gently put a hand on her leg. "You and Jayden aren't alone. You have Lil, Ryan, and me."

The little girl wrapped her good arm around

Shandra's arm and clung to her.

"Where are they?" Ryan's voice carried into the curtained area.

Mia released Shandra's arm and hopped off the table. She groaned and ran through the curtain opening.

By the time Shandra arrived in the waiting area, Ryan had picked up Mia and she was telling him all about falling off Oliver.

Ryan faced Shandra as she walked up. "Jayden?"

"He's still out. Alex can't find anything physically wrong." She grasped his free hand and he squeezed it.

"Them horses are too tall for these little ones," Lil said. Tears glistened at the corners of her eyes.

Shandra gave her friend a one arm hug.

Chandler poked his head out between the curtain. "He's coming around."

They all walked back to the bed. Jayden's eyes were open but he looked scared.

"We're here," Shandra said, walking up and taking one of his hands.

"You pulled me off of Oliver and I hurt my arm," Mia accused.

Alex parted the curtains. "It looks like everyone is here. I'm sorry but only one of you can stay while I check him out."

"Who do you want?" Shandra asked.

The boy's gaze landed on Ryan.

Shandra had thought that would be his choice. It was evident the two had had a better relationship with their father than their mother/aunt. "Come on, Mia, we'll wait out here." She took the girl from Ryan's grasp and she and Lil walked back out to the waiting room.

"I hate these places," Lil started grumbling.

"No one likes coming to an emergency room. It means something has happened to someone they love." Shandra sat, with Mia on her lap.

"You love Jayden?" the girl asked, surprise in her voice.

Shandra stared down into the child's eyes. "I love you both. You are fun, smart, and always entertaining."

"That's right," Lil said sarcastically. "Look at the fun we're having right now."

Glaring at Lil, Shandra touched Mia's nose. "What's not to love about you two?"

The child's face grew sad. "Daddy said he loves us and that Mommy would too, someday." She shook her head. "But she only ever yelled at us and told us to do things."

Keeping what she knew to herself was hard. Shandra hugged the girl the best she could without hurting her.

Ryan stepped out of the curtained area. "Alex wants to keep him for about an hour, just to make sure everything is okay. He thinks the fall just scared Jayden and knocked him out for a bit. He doesn't see any signs of concussion."

"That's good news." Shandra set Mia on her feet and stood.

"Me and Mia will take Sheba for a walk," Lil said, holding her hand out to the child.

"Thanks, Lil. You were wonderful on the mountain today." Shandra hadn't known her crusty employee could react so quickly to an accident.

"Those years traveling to rodeos with Johnny, I learned a lot about horse accidents. How to figure out what was wrong and how to fix 'em." Lil and the girl walked out of the clinic.

Ryan snapped his fingers. That was it! Andie said only a cowboy wore that type of coat. "Do they have old high school annuals in the clinic?" he asked Shandra.

She shrugged. "I don't know."

Chandler walked out of the curtained section of the ER. "Jayden would like someone to sit with him."

Shandra nodded and headed back.

"Does the clinic have past high school annuals in the waiting area?" Ryan asked the nurse.

"No. What do you want to know?" Chandler walked to the computer at the intake desk.

"I want to know if anyone connected to Mitch and Jessica Woodcock rodeoed."

Chandler grinned and started tapping on the computer keyboard. "Here's the rodeo team photos for the year Mitch and Andie graduated. You know Jessica was older?"

"Yeah." Ryan walked around and looked at the screen. He knew two of the faces staring back at him. And one had on a brown oilskin duster.

Chapter Twenty-nine

It was close to dinner time by the time Alex released Jayden. Ryan's stomach had started growling at four.

"Let's go to Maxi's and celebrate the injuries weren't any worse," Ryan suggested.

Lil glared at him. "Why would you want to take kids to a place like that?"

"It is also a restaurant, not just a bar," he argued with the woman.

Shandra put a hand on Jayden's shoulder. "Do you want to go to a restaurant or just go home?"

The boy studied each of the adults. "If Ryan wants to go to Maxi's and celebrate, I want to go there."

Ryan knew the boy would side with him. He had picked up on the fact both children had a stronger connection to him because of their connection to their father. But they were both warming to Shandra. And who wouldn't? He grinned at his wife over the tops of the children's heads.

Lil huffed, but walked with them the three blocks to Maxi's.

It was close to five by the time they arrived at the restaurant/bar.

"Oh my! What happened to you, darlin'?" Maxine asked Mia as she greeted them at the door.

"I hurt my collar and Jayden hurt his head." The girl pointed to her brother.

"Oh no! That means root beer floats on the house." Maxine led them to a booth far away from the bar and pool tables.

When they were seated and everyone had a menu, Mia asked, "What's a root beer float?"

"It's ice cream that they pour root beer, a kind of sody pop, over the top." By the look in Lil's eyes, it had been a while since she'd had the treat.

When Maxine returned with the two floats, Ryan asked her to bring another one. She returned with a third float and he motioned for her to set it in front of Lil.

The older woman's eyes went misty for a moment before she gruffly thanked Ryan.

Shandra bumped his shoulder and leaned close. "Why did you want to come here?"

He should have known his wife would know he had a motive. Otherwise, he would have suggested Ruthie's even though they had been there for lunch today. "I want to ask Maxine a couple questions. Then I'll need to visit with someone and come home later." He peered into her eyes. "And we have a lot to talk about when I get there."

She nodded, holding his gaze.

"What do y'all want for dinner?" Maxine asked, walking up to the table with an order pad.

They ordered and once she'd delivered the slip to the kitchen, Ryan walked over to the bar where the proprietress was serving drinks.

"You must be off duty, hauling children in here for dinner and coming to the bar for a drink," the woman said.

"No. Just feeding my family after a misfortune."

Her eyebrows rose. "Your family. You and Shandra taking in those two?"

"We're thinking about it. Did Richard Webb ever name who he thought his wife was fooling around with when he was in here?" Ryan kept his gaze on the woman's face.

"Last week, he came in here complaining he had to fire the best mechanic he ever had because of his wife. We all knew he meant Mitch." She leaned forward, crossing her arms on the bar and resting her ample breasts on her arms. "You mean Mitch and Della Webb were getting it on?"

He nodded. "Any chance any of your employees put two and two together? One that had a past with Mitch?"

Maxine straightened. Her tall beehive of red hair didn't even sway at the quick movement. "The few times Mitch came in here Angel was all over him. I heard they had a past." She narrowed her eyes. "You think she killed him out of jealousy?" The woman snorted very unladylike. "That woman was crazy for him. I can't see her killing him. Maybe Della, but not him."

"Thanks." Ryan returned to the table and enjoyed

dinner with his family.

~*~

After loading everyone up in Shandra's Jeep, Ryan sent them home while he wandered down to Pop's Bar. He'd called and asked for a city cop to sit across the street in case he found out enough to haul Angel in. He still needed to know where she got the poison and why she would poison Jessica. He surmised she planted the bloody jacket at Andie's to get her implicated in the murders. He could see her shooting Mitch out of jealousy. But beyond that, he had no motive for Jessica. And since they knew the murders were committed by the same person, he had to get proof.

He walked into Pop's and sat at the bar.

Steve nodded from the other end. When he finished handing out drinks, he came over. "Twice in one week. You taking up hanging out at bars?" He placed a paper coaster on the counter in front of Ryan.

"Iced tea, please." He scanned the bar. Angel was serving a group over by the pool tables.

The bartender's gaze followed his. "You still looking for who killed Mitch and Jessica?"

"I am."

"Then why are you looking at my sister?" Steve sloshed the tea over the edge of the glass, he set it down so hard.

"I'm just piecing things together. You and your sister knew the victims. I'm trying to find a motive for Jessica's death." Ryan picked up the tea and sipped.

"How did she die? I'm guessing it wasn't suicide like we first heard." The bartender waved off a man trying to get his attention.

"Poison. Monkshood to be precise."

Steve flinched. He knew the flower and the poison.

"What do you know about the poison?" Ryan studied him.

"Jessica told us about it when we were in high school. I was complaining about the mice getting into my horse's grain in our tack room. She suggested using Monkshood to kill the mice. Her mom knew a lot about herbs. Do you think she poisoned herself?" Steve asked.

Ryan shook his head. "The killer gave her a blade with the poison on it, and either forced her to cut herself or talked her into cutting her wrists."

Steve ran a hand over his face. "Jessica was getting turned around. She'd quit taking drugs. I could see it when we met." He scanned the room.

Ryan noticed he was locating his sister.

"Jess and I were going to leave. She knew Mitch was fooling around. She said she had a plan to get the money we needed to get out of this county." He waved a hand. "I didn't want this place. Never did. But what does my old man do? He puts this ball and chain around my neck and tells me it would be a good way to keep Angel out of trouble. He put all that on my shoulders the day he died of a heart attack."

Ryan caught a glimpse of Angel walking back to the bar with empty glasses as his phone buzzed. He glanced down at the text from Cathleen. He had her.

"Table eight needs refills," Angel said, staring at her brother. She faced Ryan. "What have you been telling him? He looks like he lost his best friend."

Steve slapped a hand on the counter. "I did!"

She laughed. "She was only your friend until she found something better. Just like her sister."

"Jessica and I were going to leave this place. You

would have had all of this to yourself." Steve braced his hands on the counter as if keeping himself from reaching across and grabbing his sister by the neck.

"She would have dumped you for the first person who came along with drugs or more money." Angel stomped a booted foot. "She wasn't worth your time."

"And you made sure of it," Ryan said in a normal voice.

The woman narrowed her eyes. "What are you talking about?"

"Sunday, when the kids told Jessica their father was dead, she called here."

"When?" Steve asked. "I didn't get a call from her."

"I'm guessing she left a message. One saying Mitch was dead and she was ready to get out of here. Asking you to come to the house and work things out." Ryan kept his gaze on Angel. "Only your sister heard the message, erased it, and put a plan in motion she'd been planning for a while."

"I don't know what you're talking about," Angel said.

"First, she took your only love, Mitch, and now she was going to take your brother. You couldn't have that could you?" Ryan glanced at Steve. He had disbelief and grief on his face.

"She didn't deserve anything. Not Mitch, not the kids, not my brother. Nothing."

Ryan grabbed Angel by the arm, leading her to the door. He had a suspicion if he didn't get her apprehended, she'd take off. "You'll need to find another barmaid."

"What are you doing? You can't drag me out of

work and not tell me why?" Angel dug in with her feet.

"I suspect you of murdering Mitch and Jessica Woodcock."

The woman still had her feet dragging but she'd clamped her mouth closed. Ryan led her over to the city cop car and put her in the back seat.

"Ow, stop shoving," Angel said, putting an arm to her hip as though staving off pain.

"Take her to the station, put her in an interview room, and get a female to take a photo of the bruise on her right hip area."

When the car pulled away, he walked back into the bar.

Steve's face was red with rage. "Why the hell did you drag her out of here?"

"Because she killed Mitch and Jessica. I just need to get all the proof. Do you think she had any idea you and Jessica were planning to leave before the message Sunday?" Ryan sat back down. His iced tea was still sitting where he'd left it. He took a sip, waiting for the man to calm down and think.

"She did start acting angry with me after Jerry Parson was in here one night."

"What would Parson have to do with Jessica and you?" Ryan's thoughts went to the box of meth under her rose bush.

"She wouldn't tell me exactly how she was getting the money to leave, but I know it had to do with Jerry. He might have said something about me and Jessica leaving once she did whatever it was for him." Steve stared at the counter. "You really think Angel killed both of them?"

"She'd learned that Mitch was having an affair

with Della Webb. At the cabin where Mitch was killed. Had she been to the cabin before?"

"Lots of times when she and Mitch were dating. That cabin has belonged to his family forever."

"That's something else. Why haven't his parents shown up to take the kids? I would have thought with Mitch gone, they would want his offspring." Ryan had thought the grandparents would have arrived by now and want the twins. If it were his parents, they would have been back here the next day and swooped in to take care of their grandchildren.

"They were never really hands-on parents. It was teachers and other people who got Mitch that football scholarship. The best thing he ever did was the twins. And it was the worst thing that could have happened to Jessica. She didn't want them. I never did understand how she could talk so poorly of her own kids."

Ryan kept the information he knew to himself. It wasn't his to tell. "Does your sister know how to shoot a shotgun?"

"She's shot one a time or two. But she doesn't have one." He finally went down the bar to serve people.

He needed to talk to Parson. Ryan pulled out his phone and called dispatch. "Have whoever is out in the vicinity of Jerry Parson tomorrow morning, bring him in for questioning."

Placing a five-dollar bill on the counter by his drink, Ryan walked out to his vehicle. He called dispatch again and asked for a deputy to pick up Angel Ervin at the Huckleberry police station and hold her overnight at the county jail in Warner for suspicion of murder. He hoped by morning he had enough proof to arrest her for the two homicides.

Chapter Thirty

Waiting for Ryan, Shandra sat down on the couch. She wondered what he had discovered at Maxi's. He'd had a lengthy conversation with the owner and came back to the table looking confident. But they hadn't had time alone for him to tell her what he'd discovered.

It had taken longer to get the two children settled in for the night. It was Jayden's turn to have Sheba. The boy had wrapped his arms around the mutt and fell to sleep quickly, while Mia had trouble getting comfortable. Shandra finally broke down and gave the child the aspirin Alex told her to use if Mia's pain worsened. She didn't like giving medicine to children.

The chamomile tea slowly relaxed her and she drifted off to sleep.

Ella stood in between Mia and Jayden. She was smiling and pointing to what looked like a bear. Shandra joined them. When she opened her mouth to question, her grandmother shook her head.

The brown body went from being hunched over to standing. Blonde hair cascaded down the animal's back. Following the flow of hair with her gaze, Shandra saw a hand, dripping with blood. She spun to question Ella and realized the children were frightened. She gathered them to her. "It's okay. No one will hurt you."

A noise woke Shandra.

She sat up and listened.

Familiar footsteps in the hall. Ryan was home.

She slid her legs over the edge of the couch as he entered the great room.

"You didn't need to wait up," he said, crossing to her. "I looked in on the kids. They're sound asleep."

"It took Mia a while. Her collar bone was hurting." Shandra stretched. "I just had a dream."

Ryan sat down next to her. "What about?"

"I think Mia and Jayden saw who killed their mother. It was a person in the brown coat that they saw in the trees at the cabin. A woman with blonde hair." Shandra could tell this information about the woman wasn't new to him.

"I have Angel Ervin in custody. I plan to talk to her in the morning. If I can't get her to talk, I can setup a line up for the kids to pick her out of." He shook his head. "I just don't want to put them through that."

"I don't want to either. Let's hope she confesses in the morning."

~*~

After making sure the kids were bouncing back from their fall the day before, Ryan headed to Warner. On the way he called the District Attorney to fill him in on what he suspected. He requested a warrant to search

Angel's vehicle and residence for anything that might tie her to the deaths. The other request was also granted. The DA gave him the green light to give Jerry Parson immunity for anything he said about the meth he distributed if he had information that would help convict Angel Ervin. In a week or so, he could have the State Police do a sweep of the county looking for drugs and Meth houses.

Cathleen glanced up when he walked into the Sheriff's Office. She stepped out of her cubicle. "How are the kids?"

"Fine. Mia dislocated her collar bone and Jayden was knocked out for a bit, but they seem to be fine this morning."

"Kids are like that." She patted his arm and went back to her desk.

Ryan noted a deputy standing at an interview room door. "Is that Parson?"

The deputy nodded. "He looked a little gray when Deputy Speaks brought him in."

"He probably thinks we hauled him in about the drugs. Thanks." Ryan passed the interview room and into his office. He checked for any new emails from forensics and picked up the two files on the murders.

Stepping into the interview room, he smiled.

Parson narrowed his eyes. "You narcotics, too?"

Ryan shook his head, sat, and started the recording device. "This is your lucky day, Mr. Parson. The DA is willing to give you a pass this time on the drugs if you can tell me why Jessica Woodcock was keeping a box full of meth under her rosebush when she was cleaning up her act?"

The man relaxed and leaned back in the chair. "I

was paying her to keep it hidden. I'd discovered when I'd come back from walks with the boys that I'd have a pack or two missing. Someone had been coming in and stealing from me. So when I'd walk to Jessica's, I'd give her the bags and she'd hide them. I didn't know where. Didn't want to know. She'd have whatever amount I needed to sell to a buyer all wrapped up in paper bags when I'd drop by to pick it up."

"Why did you trust a drug user to take care of your product?" That didn't make any sense to him.

The man stared at him. "Because she wanted something more than she wanted drugs-freedom. All she talked about was getting away from this county, her husband, and the brats." Parson scratched his head. "Never did understand why she hated those kids. They were her own flesh and blood. Maybe it was because they tied her to Mitch, but she could have divorced and let him have custody of them."

Ryan nodded. She could have left at any time. Why hadn't she? Still feeling she needed to watch over her sister? They would never know why she didn't just walk away.

"Did you mention paying Jessica so she could leave town to anyone?" Ryan hadn't mentioned anywhere or a certain person to see if he could incriminate Angel.

"I might have said something to a couple people. Mind you, they were people that wouldn't say anything about how I make extra money." He almost pulled off an apologetic expression. Almost.

"Who were they?" Ryan persisted. He needed to show Angel knew her brother and Jessica were leaving. He had to prove jealousy and a grudge had made her snap.

"I remember sitting in Pop's one evening. I think it was a Saturday night. Yeah, it was. I'd met—never mind who I'd met. I saw Jessica walk in, kind of nod to Steve, and then go back out the door. A few minutes later Steve disappeared.

Angel was behind the bar, fuming about how it was just like Steve to run out of something when the bar was busy. I said it looked to me like he was meeting Jessica. She cussed, slammed some glasses around, and then asked me how I knew that. I told her what I saw and she slapped the rag in her hand onto the bar and walked into the back.

The next time I visited with Jessica, I asked her if she and Steve were an item. She just smiled and said, soon. I put two and two together. But all I said after that to Angel was not to worry, Jessica was leaving."

Ryan nodded. "And when was this?"

"Last week sometime. Can't remember exactly."

"Thank you." Ryan stood.

"I can go, now?"

"As soon as a deputy gets you to sign your statement."

Ryan stepped out of the room. "When he signs his statement, he's free to go."

The deputy nodded.

Ryan walked into his office.

Deputy Trapp was sitting in a chair. The grin on his face said he'd found something either in Angel's vehicle or home.

"What did you find?"

"There were bloody smears in the carpet of the trunk of her car. Sent those to forensics along with a small bottle of liquid. And, per your suggestion, I took the mug shot of your suspect to the hardware store that said a woman came in wanting to buy two shotgun shells. He said your suspect was the one. He sold her a box of double-aught cartridges. I found the box- minus one shell and the receipt in the trunk of the car."

Ryan thumped the files still in his hands. "We got her."

Chapter Thirty-one

Shandra stood in her kitchen handing dishes to her sisters-in-law and mother-in-law to take out to the barbecue happening on their back patio. Ryan's family, all three siblings, nieces and nephews, and his parents, along with Maxwell, Ruthie, and Donnie, and Alex and Miranda had been invited to celebrate Jayden and Mia joining the family.

The adoption wouldn't be final for a year, but the process had been started. The DNA results had come back matching Jessica as a family member but not a parent. They had known that from Andie's confirmation. However, they had no idea who their father could be. Mitch didn't match any of the characteristics in the children. It appeared their mother had more than one secret she was holding onto. Shandra and Ryan had decided the children didn't need to know any different. If, when they were older, they wanted to know more, they could seek it on their own.

Shandra still wondered at Andie being so adamant she didn't want her children. Was it because she feared her husband would find out Mitch hadn't been the father and she'd tricked him? How far back did the woman's deceit go? She shook her head. They may never know why the woman was adamant the children were Mitch and Jessica's.

Ryan had made Andie talk to the kids and explain that she was really their mother and that she had known as soon as she was pregnant, she wouldn't be a good mother. She'd hoped her sister, who had taken such good care of her would do the same for them.

The twins now understood why the person they called Mommy hadn't treated them like one. But they were still confused as to why their real mother didn't want them. Mitch's parents said they loved being grandparents but didn't want to be parents again. All of the twin's next of kin gave them up for adoption.

"Come on. You're missing all the fun," Miranda said, waddling into the kitchen, her hands on her protruding stomach.

Shandra grinned. "I don't want to do that."

Out on the patio, the twins were getting to know their new cousins. The women sat in chairs, drinks in their hands, visiting and instructing the men how to barbecue the chicken and hamburgers.

Standing at the edge of all the merriment, Shandra felt complete for the first time in a very long time. This was family. Her family. Not all of it, of course. They had a trip planned next month to visit her family at the Reservation. So they could meet Mia and Jayden.

Honking at the front of the house caused everyone

to jump up. Kids ran around the side of the house yelling at one another to see who it was.

Ryan grasped Shandra's hand and they walked with the rest of the adults to the front.

Lil stepped out of her pickup, hooked up to the horse trailer. She'd told Shandra this morning she'd be back for the party but had to go pick up a horse she'd bought.

Shandra had been happy Lil had moved on from Sunshine's passing.

The older woman called out, "Mia and Jayden, I need help."

The twins ran to the back of the trailer.

"I don't see a horse in there?" Ryan said.

"Me either." Shandra wondered what the woman was up to.

The trailer door opened and Mia let out a joyful screech. Lil stepped inside and stepped out leading two Welch ponies. One was black and the other a palomino.

"Meet Cookie and Cream," Lil said, handing the black pony to Jayden and the palomino to Mia.

"For us?" Mia exclaimed.

"I don't want you two riding a horse you can't get on and off of by yourself. When you outgrow these then you can have a real horse." Lil motioned to the corral. "Go on, put them in the little gathering pen and feed them."

The two led the ponies with all their new cousins following them.

Shandra walked up to Lil and hugged her. "You didn't have to do that."

Lil had tears in her eyes. "I wanted to. Them two deserve every darn thing we can give them."

"Do I smell something burning?" Colleen, Ryan's mother, asked.

The men took off running to the back of the house and the women stood out front laughing.

About the Author

Thank you for reading ***Capricious Demise.*** I enjoyed bringing new family members into the Higheagle-Greer family.

I hope you will continue to follow Shandra and Ryan's investigations. I will continue to write their stories as long as I can come up with believable, interesting murders.

If you enjoyed this book, please leave a review. It is the best way to thank an author for an enjoyable read. I love to hear from fans.

All my work has Western or Native American elements in them along with hints of humor and engaging characters. My husband and I raise alfalfa hay in rural eastern Oregon. Riding horses and battling rattlesnakes, I not only write the western lifestyle, I live it.

If you like the Shandra Higheagle Mysteries, you might like my Gabriel Hawke Novels. Check them out at my website.

Website: http://www.patyjager.net
Blog: https://writingintothesunset.net/
FB Page: https://www.facebook.com/PatyJagerAuthor/
Amazon: https://www.amazon.com/Paty-Jager/e/B002I7M0VK
Pinterest: https://www.pinterest.com/patyjag/
Twitter: https://twitter.com/patyjag
Goodreads: http://www.goodreads.com/author/show/1005334.Paty_Jager

Thank you for purchasing this Windtree Press publication.
For other books of the heart, please visit our website
at www.windtreepress.com.

For questions or more information contact us
at info@windtreepress.com.

Windtree Press
www.windtreepress.com

Hillsboro, OR 97124

www.ingramcontent.com/pod-product-compliance
Lightning Source LLC
Chambersburg PA
CBHW070936190726
48292CB00004B/1200

Shandra Higheagle Mystery Books

Double Duplicity

Tarnished Remains

Deadly Aim

Murderous Secrets

Killer Descent

Reservation Revenge

Yuletide Slaying

Fatal Fall

Haunting Corpse

Artful Murder

Dangerous Dance

Homicide Hideaway

Toxic Trigger-point

Abstract Casualty